THE DUCHESS PULLS A FAST ONE
THE COMPLETE CASES OF THE DUCHESS

THE

THE DUCHESS PULLS A FAST ONE
THE COMPLETE CASES OF THE DUCHESS

WHITMAN CHAMBERS

PRIMARY ILLUSTRATOR
JOSEPH A. FARREN

COVER BY
JOHN ATHERTON

POPULAR PUBLICATIONS · 2022

TABLE OF CONTENTS

THE DUCHESS SPOTS A KILLER

*Pinky Kane, Spike Kaylor and the
Beautiful Katie Blayne Join Forces to Trap
a Master Criminal, with Results that
are Highly Disturbing to One Reporter's
Heart and a Killer's Perfect Alibi*

AS I WALKED into the City Hall press room that afternoon Spike Kaylor had evidently just hit the ceiling and come down with feet spread, fists clenched and eyes shooting fire.

"All right, you lugs!" he bellowed, glaring around the room. "Who took it?"

Willie Blake of the *Sentinel*, Pete Zerker, who works for the *Bulletin*, and Slim Lonergan went on with their card game. Katie Blayne, blond and slim and lovely, who covers day police for the *Sun*, proceeded calmly with the business of making up her lips.

Spike aimed a kick at the waste basket. "If this is an act," he roared, "you yokels can ring down the lousy curtain!… Who took it?"

Everybody remained very busy.

I said mildly to my co-worker on the *Telegram:* "Who took what?"

"Why, my new overcoat," he indignantly replied. "I leave it hanging there on a hook by the washbowl. I run up to the mayor's office for a chat. I come back and it's gone."

Well, there was something queer about it. This was October in California. Overcoats, for such hardy souls as Spike Kaylor, were still in mothballs. And as for a new overcoat—Spike's salary, by his own confession, was more than a week overdrawn.

"Come on, you muggs!" Spike stormed. "Kick in! Where's my overcoat?"

Pete Zerker, his long face singularly like that of a tired truck horse, looked up from his cards. "This, Mr. Kaylor, is a press room," he pointed out. "The checking concession has not yet been farmed out. Until it is, are we to be

"I thought you newspaper guys weren't supposed to play cards till after three o'clock," Jake Morris jeered.

responsible for such miscellaneous articles of wearing apparel as you choose—"

"Oh, skip it! Who was in here while I was upstairs?"

Willie pursed his lips. "Let me see—"

"Duchess!" Spike snapped.

Katie closed her compact and looked up, smiling. "Yes—darling!"

"Who was in here during the half hour I was talking to the mayor?"

"Why, at least a dozen people dropped in, Spike," she replied, and then added, "mostly cops."

"That's a lot of help," Spike groaned.

I said, "Look here, guy. If the question isn't out of order, may I ask where you got a new overcoat?"

Spike looked vaguely foolish. "What in Sam Hill has that got to do with it?"

"Your young cohort," Pete Zerker told me, "has been indulging his well-known predilection for crap shooting."

"Spike," said Willie Blake, "was down in the bull pen this morning shooting crap with the city's guests."

"Yes," said the Duchess brightly, "Spike won a beautiful camel's hair overcoat from—"

"Of all people," Pete Zerker said indignantly.

"A burglar," Katie finished.

Spike flushed, growling: "There's no law against it, is there?"

"There are plenty of laws against it," I said, "but don't worry about them. Who is this burglar you won the coat from?"

"A punk by the name of Dopey McClain. Held in five grand bail for a job in Leona Heights."

"And where is Dopey McClain now?"

"Last I saw of him he was back in his cell. The turnkey caught us just after I'd won the overcoat and locked the whole gang up again." Spike grinned reminiscently. "Almost locked me up, too."

"We," said Willie Blake, "would have been saved a lot of grief if he had."

"Spike, you poor sap!" I said. "Hasn't it penetrated your thick cranium that this guy has made bail and walked calmly in here and reclaimed his coat?"

"What guy has made bail, huh?"

We all turned and there stood big Jake Morris, who had slipped into the room without, as usual, a sound. Jake looks like he was raised in a dark cellar. He is as offensive as one of those gray bugs you find when you turn over a board. But Jake was one of our crosses. He wrote bail bonds and we had to tolerate him. A bail bond broker can break more news than six chiefs of police.

"Here," I said, "is the so-and-so in the woodpile."

"I ain't been in no woodpile," Jake said virtuously, "and I ain't no so-and-so. What guy were you talkin' about made bail, huh?"

"A guy by the name of Dopey McClain. How about it, Jake?"

"Sure. I wrote his bond," answered Jake.

"When?" Spike demanded.

Jake looked up at the clock; it was eight minutes of three. "If I remember correct, Dopey was released at two-forty. I think that's what it says on the blotter."

Spike gasped. "That damned punk must have just slipped by me in the hall. All right, Jake. Where is he?"

"Should I know where he is?"

"Now don't be funny. You're not going to write a five-grand bond on a burglar and then turn him loose to skip on you. Where you got him stowed away?"

Jake grinned and turned out his coat pockets. "I swear it, Spike. I ain't got the faintest idea where he is."

Spike groaned and sat down, wiping the perspiration off his face with a soiled handkerchief. "A swell bunch of pals you turned out to be," he said bitterly.

Jake chuckled; he sounded as though he were trying to cough a fish bone out of his throat. He looked at the card players. "I thought you newspaper guys weren't supposed to play cards till after three o'clock," he jeered.

"What's three o'clock got to do with it?" I asked.

Pete Zerker looked up. "You haven't heard the Chief's latest, Pinky. Newspaper men assigned to the City Hall will refrain from playing cards in the press room until after three o'clock. We're breaking rules for the fun of it."

"The hell you say! What's the bright idea?"

All eyes turned to Katie.

"Well, Duchess?" I said.

"It was the Lady's suggestion, Pinky."

She referred to Miss Jane Tobin, the hell-roaring, two-fisted city editor of the *Sun*. It was Miss Tobin who, a few months before, had sent Katie Blayne over to cover police. And it was Katie Blayne who, serene and beautiful and disgustingly competent, had not only seriously cramped our style but had put over a number of important news beats on us.

"I see," I replied heavily. "Miss Tobin, besides running the *Sun* these days, is now trying to take the directorship of the press room."

"That's about it, Pinky," the Duchess nodded, smiling.

"I ask again, what's the bright idea?"

"Card games draw so many bums." She looked straight at big Jake Morris. "And bums, hanging around all the time, interfere with my work."

Jake bristled. "I like that. A bum, huh? I'm a bum, huh?"

"Sing it, Jake," Katie said pleasantly.

Jake gurgled.

"All right, Duchess," I said. "Have it your way. You and the Lady keep on. You'll lead with your right once too often."

"And then?"

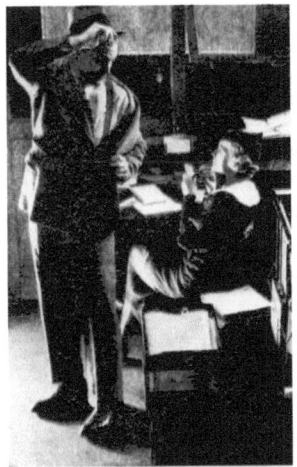

"Duchess, you stay here. This may get rough."

"We'll hang one on you," I said viciously, "that'll put you to sleep for a week."

Pete Zerker said, "It seems to me, Pinky, that you and Spike have been making that threat for a long time."

"Go fry your mush, Pete!" I snapped. And to Jake! "Come on, Jake, deal 'em."

"Okay."

I jerked over a chair and sat down. Jake set a flask of whiskey on the desk and picked up a deck of cards.

The others went back to their card game. Jake and I sat down to a two-handed game of pinochle. Katie went out, conjured a story from some one, and phoned it to her office on her private line. Spike Kaylor sulked in a corner, occasionally passing a remark about his pals who had let a burglar walk into the room and steal his overcoat.

It was all pretty dull. Cordially disliking Jake Morris, bored by the rest, I didn't get much kick out of the game. It was four o'clock and I'd about decided to call it off and go to a movie—I wasn't due to take over the beat from Spike until six—when we got the flash.

Slim Jenkins, one of the dicks on the pawn shop detail, poked his head into the room.

"Hey, you guys! Want a swell murder?"

Did we want a swell murder!

"Al Rosenblatt. You know, the diamond importer. Office

in the McDonald Building. They just found him. Brains scattered all over the floor. Safe open and cleaned. Thought you'd like to know."

Would we like to know!

We went out of there like a string of apparatus on a three-alarm fire. And left big Jake calling, "Hey! You owe me four bits. Hey, Pink!"

Spike and I, Willie and Zerker shot across the street and down the block to the McDonald Building, an ancient three-story structure which had somehow been overlooked when progress marched across the downtown district. As we were clattering up the stairs I realized all at once that Katie was right on our heels.

I stopped, swung around, blocked her path.

"Look, kid! You don't want to see this. It'll be a mess. Why drag along? You haven't an edition for a couple of hours. Go back to the hall and get the story from the dicks."

"Pinky, Pinky," she said sadly, breathlessly. "Do you really think I'm too soft to look at a dead man?"

"You're not soft, Katie. You can take 'em as they come. But why go out of your way to look at a thing like this?"

"Because I want all the details for my paper. And I can't count on anybody to give them to me."

Well, she'd been fighting us for a long time, a lone girl against four men. I wondered if she wasn't getting a bit tired of carrying the ball for the *Sun*.

"You can count on me, kid," I told her. "I'll give you all the dope. I'm not officially on the job till six, you know, and Spike Kaylor will have to—"

"Thanks, Pinky," she interrupted. Her blue eyes were

steady as they met mine, and her voice was cool. "I'll go upstairs now, please. If you'll stand aside."

"Oh. So you don't trust me."

"Not even a little bit, Pinky," she said quietly.

"All right, Duchess. To hell with you!"

I ran on up the stairs, boiling.

AL ROSENBLATT, THE diamond merchant, had a single room on the third floor, one of the few offices now occupied in this ramshackle building. Bodie Wallis, Captain of Detectives, and Pete Moran, head of the homicide detail, were in charge and a harness bull stood on guard at the door.

We all flashed our press cards and went in. The room was large and was furnished with a desk, several chairs, a big square table in the center and an old-fashioned safe in the far corner. The door of the safe was open and between it and the table was the body of Al Rosenblatt.

The diamond merchant lay on his back, one leg drawn under him, both arms raised as though he had been shielding his head when he fell. His dull eyes, wide with the terror which had gripped him, stared up at the ceiling. His bald head was a bloody mess. The top of the skull had been caved in with a jack handle which, wrapped with a bloodstained rag, lay beside the body.

"Like it, Duchess?" I asked Katie in an undertone.

"Love it." Her whisper was resolute, but her face was dead white and she held her lips tight to keep them from trembling. Captain Wallis was questioning a slight, middle-aged man who stood by the table mopping his gray-green face.

"Have you touched anything, Mr. Rosenblatt?"

The sweating man said: "Not a thing except the telephone, Captain. As soon as I forced the lock and got in I
called police headquarters. I didn't even touch my—the
body. I knew my father was dead."

"Now let's go over this again. You say it's your custom to
call for your father every afternoon at three-thirty?"

"Yes, sir. He wasn't well and kept short office hours. He
had no car of his own and didn't care for taxis, so I made a
point of calling for him and taking him home."

"And today you came and found the door locked and
got no answer when you knocked."

"Yes."

"You suspected something was wrong and broke the
lock." Captain Wallis looked at the door and back again
at the little man, skeptically.

"Yes. The lock gave quite easily. The building is old, you
know."

"Yes, I know." Wallis looked down at the dead man.
"Was your father in the habit of keeping any great number
of diamonds in that old safe?"

"No. He kept his diamonds in a safety deposit vault. But
when he expected a customer he went out and got them
and put them in the safe. He never left any gems there
overnight."

Captain Wallis nodded and strolled to the desk, while
Rosenblatt folded limply into a chair. The captain, with
something of the air of a pouncing cat, picked up a memo-
randum pad. He read:

"Frank Leopold. Three p.m. Two-three carat." He looked
over his shoulder at Rosenblatt. "Did your father do busi-

ness with Frank Leopold?" Leopold is one of the city's leading jewelers.

"No. Not for two years. They had an argument over some stones."

Wallis grunted. "Then how come, do you suppose, Frank Leopold made an appointment with your father for 3 p.m. to look at some two- and three-carat diamonds?"

"I can't understand that, Captain. I didn't think Leopold would ever do business with my father again."

Pete Moran, who had been kneeling beside the body, jumped up excitedly. He held out a watch, exclaimed: "Look, Captain! Stopped at 3:01."

Wallis took the watch, turned it over in his palm, nodded thoughtfully.

"Get it?" Moran asked, bubbling with eagerness.

"I think so." The Captain laid the watch on the table and stood for a moment surveying the scene. "It was like this. Some one came here to look at diamonds. Rosenblatt opened his safe and when he turned from it he was tapped on the head. He fell forward, as a man does when he's knocked cold. In falling he hit the corner of the table with his chest. That caved in the back of his watch and stopped it."

"And fixed the time of the killing," Moran put in, hurriedly, "at exactly 3:01."

"Yes. And in striking the corner of the table that way, Rosenblatt spun around so that he fell on his back. The killer proceeded to finish him where he lay, rifle the safe, set the catch on the door and lam out of here."

Captain Wallis paused and looked sharply at the little man in the chair. He asked, very casually:

"Where, Mr. Rosenblatt, were you at three o'clock this afternoon?"

Rosenblatt gulped. His jaw dropped and he stared blankly at Wallis for a moment. "Why I—I was in my office. I'm an attorney, you know."

The Captain's voice was a bit sharper. "Yes, I know that. Who was with you in your office from, say, two-thirty until you came up here at three-thirty?… Come, come! Who was with you there? Anybody?"

"Y-y-es. Certainly." Rosenblatt got hold of himself. "From two-thirty to three-thirty I was conferring with three of my clients. I see what you're driving at, Captain, but you're off on the wrong foot. I have a perfect alibi. Three of the most prominent men in this city were with—"

"Let it pass!" Wallis barked. "Moran, get Frank Leopold on the phone and tell him to report to headquarters immediately. As for you fellows"—he looked around at us—"you ought to have your story, so suppose you clear out and give us a chance to go over this room properly."

I said quickly: "May we look at that watch, Captain?"

"Have it your way, Duchess," I said, "but you and the Lady will lead with the right once too often."

"Sure. Go ahead."

I went over to the table and picked up the timepiece. It was an octagonal Hamilton of fairly recent vintage. Though the crystal was unbroken, the hands had stopped at 3:01. Turning it over, I saw that the case was engraved with the initials "A.Z.R." in block letters. The back of the watch was jammed in with a very definite impression; Rosenblatt had evidently struck the corner of the table with considerable force when he fell.

Willie and Zerker had already dashed for a telephone to catch their Final Nights with the story. Spike and Katie looked at the watch and then the three of us started back to the press room together. When we got out of the building, Spike said, "well, how about it?"

I thought for a minute. "The son's alibi was too damned pat."

"Did that strike you, too?" Spike asked quickly.

"It struck me right between the eyes. How about you?"

"It practically knocked me for a loop. Soon as he began to beef about three of the most prominent men in the city, I tumbled."

I took Katie's arm as we started to cross the street to the City Hall. She didn't exactly pull away from me, but she kept her distance.

"Are you two nitwits suggesting," she asked witheringly, "that that little man killed his father?"

Spike slapped her on the back, not gently. "Nice work, Duchess. How'd you ever tumble? I tell you, kid. You string along with us and you'll be a reporter some day."

"Some day!" she retorted. "String along with you and I'll get scooped every day."

"You know all the by-God answers, don't you?" Spike jeered.

"Most of them," Katie flashed. "But seriously. You don't really think Rosenblatt killed his father, do you? Good heavens, what was his motive?"

"A fortune in ice."

"Nonsense!" the Duchess snapped. "The old man must have been close to seventy. Why kill him? The son was bound to come into the diamonds before long anyway."

"Are you quite sure of that, Duchess? Perhaps the old guy had cut the son out of his will."

"All right, all right," Katie said wearily. "Have it your way. You usually do and you're usually wrong."

We went into the press room and found Jake Morris still at the desk, riffling the cards. Spike and Katie hit their telephones with a flash and I sat down across from Jake.

"Dead?" Jake asked.

"Like a mackerel."

"Good."

I glanced at him. His fat, slightly greasy face had the greenish-yellow tinge of a parsnip. And I thought: A reporter's life isn't all gin and ginger ale when we have to associate with worms like Jake Morris.

"Friend of yours, huh?" I said.

"We was pardners in the diamond racket for fifteen years."

"Sure. I remember now. You pulled out three or four years ago and started writing bail bonds. Tell me, Jake. How many times did you have to hit him?"

"To kill him, you mean?"

"Yes."

Jake chuckled in that offensive way he has, as though something were lodged in his throat. "Oh, eight or ten times, I guess." He put the cards down. "Tell me about it."

I told him the story briefly and asked: "What do you think of his son?"

"Newman? A shyster and a rat."

"Think he may have had a hand in it?"

"Me, I wouldn't be surprised if he had both feet in it. He'd cut his grandmother's throat for four bits, that guy."

"He has an alibi."

"Sure. So did Hauptmann."

KATIE AND SPIKE joined us after a while and we sat around talking over the murder. Willie Blake came in finally with word that Frank Leopold was in the dicks' office. The jeweler swore he had made no appointment with Rosenblatt.

"He has four clerks in his establishment," Willie told us, "and he says they'll all testify he was in the store at three o'clock. He's clear, I guess. Somebody evidently used his name to make an appointment, not knowing he and Rosenblatt were at outs."

Pete Zerker came in a few minutes later. "Newman Rosenblatt is getting an order to open his old man's safety deposit box. Newman says the loss may run better than a hundred thousand dollars."

And that was that—for a while.

"COME ON, SPIKE," I suggested. "Let's go out and get a load of Java. You have plenty of time before the first run."

We crossed the street to Joe's lunch room and went inside. There was a fellow sitting at the counter with a cup of coffee in one hand and a wedge of pie in the other. He wore a beautiful mauve-gray camel's-hair overcoat.

"Well!" Spike bellowed abruptly. "My friend, the burglar."

The fellow looked up. "Hello, pal," he said cheerfully. "How's the newspaper racket?"

"Great—pal," Spike retorted. "How's the prowl racket?"

"Not so bad, not so bad."

"Nice coat you picked up there."

"Yeah," Dopey McClain agreed, squirming. "Quite a coat, pal."

"Take it off!"

"Huh?"

"I said, take it off."

"You ain't goin' to snag the coat off a poor guy's back, are you," Dopey pleaded.

"Watch me!"

Spike reached for him.

"Wait! Wait" Dopey dropped his coffee and pie and reached for his pockets. "Got a few knick-knacks. Cigarettes, one thing 'n another."

"My cigarettes" Spike snorted.

He caught hold of the coat's lapels and peeled the garment neatly off Dopey's back. He climbed into it, shrugged the padded shoulders into place and sat down on a stool two removed from the burglar.

"And I thought you was my pal," Dopey moaned.

"Yeah? Maybe I thought the same about you. So what?"

Dopey shrugged, grinned. "The chow's on me, boys. Eat up."

Well, the burglar paid for our coffee, and we told him to keep out of jail and strolled back to the press room.

Pete Zerker and Willie Blake, the afternoon paper men, had seen their sheet to bed and gone home. Katie was alone and she looked pretty white. I think she was having a hard time forgetting Al Rosenblatt's bashed and bloody head.

"Look, Spike," I said. "You got a bottle of whiskey in your locker. Give the child a shot."

"Whiskey for this infant? Mother's milk is more in her line."

I went over to Spike's locker and brought the Duchess a drink. She accepted it wordlessly. For an instant her fine blue eyes met mine and I felt my heart flutter as it had of late whenever she looked at me. Then she downed her drink and said:

"Thanks—darling."

And I said, "You're not any too damned welcome—dear!"

And I hated her again, and wished she'd go back where she belonged, to reporting golden weddings and births of triplets.

I turned away and saw Spike standing in the center of the room, his hands thrust in the pockets of his overcoat, a look of shocked surprise on his homely face.

"Spill it, guy," I ordered.

He slowly withdrew his right hand from his pocket. He opened it and stared at a neat gold watch. I laughed.

"Your dinger is also a pickpocket. Quite an accomplished young man."

"But not much of a crap shooter," Katie said.

"Now what?" asked Spike. "If I turn it in and tell where I got it, it means the Big House for my pal, the burglar. On the other hand, if I keep it and somebody recognizes it—"

"Whoever lost it will beef to the cops," I pointed out. "Watch the reports and mail it back anonymously to the owner. How's that?"

Spike sighed. "Oh, that's oke, I guess," he said sadly. "But it's a hell of a swell watch."

Katie had stiffened a little. "May I see it?" she asked.

She took the ticker and held it out in the palm of her hand. It was a beautiful hand, with slender, tapering fingers. I was much more interested in it than in the watch. I saw her turn the latter over and look at the engraving on the back. Even then I didn't tumble, for it was perhaps the first time I'd ever noticed how lovely Katie's hands are.

The Duchess returned the ticker and stood looking from Spike to me. Her lips curled with a fine contempt.

"Just a pair of bright reporters," she said scathingly. "You'll go a long way, you two—in the wrong direction."

"All right, Duchess!" Spike snapped. "Commence!"

"Look at the watch."

"I've looked at it. I think it's a swell watch. What's the add? Kick in, Duchess?"

"Look at it again."

"You want me to get eye-strain? Spill it, kid!"

"Hasn't it occurred to you," Katie retorted contemptuously, "that that watch is a twin of the one Pete Moran took out of old Mr. Rosenblatt's vest pocket?"

Spike looked at the watch, shrugging. "And so?" he sneered. "Must I get into a lather over it? Sister, aren't you bright enough to know that there are probably a thousand tickers just like this scattered over the city?"

Katie asked, heavily sarcastic: "With the initials A.Z.R. engraved in block letters on the case?"

"Huh?" Spike gulped. "Whazat?"

I gulped myself as I tore the watch out of Spike's fingers and stared at it.

"My God, Katie, you're right!"

"Thank you. Had you suspected I didn't know my alphabet?"

Spike sat down weakly, as though some one had stuck a pin in him and let out all his air. I sat down too, feeling suddenly faint. Only Katie remained placid, looking from Spike to me, smiling her cool and imperturbable smile. After several minutes Spike said feebly:

"Duchess, you better tell us. We haven't got brains enough to figure it out for ourselves. Shoot, kid!"

The Duchess bowed. Was she enjoying herself at our expense, or was she?

"Stop me whenever you think I'm wrong," she said quietly. "That watch belonged to Mr. Rosenblatt and was in his pocket when he was murdered. Right?"

"So right, Duchess, I'm nauseated to think how dumb I am," Spike said sadly.

"The watch which Pete Moran found in the murdered man's vest pocket was prepared by the murderer, set at 3:01, and the back caved in and the watch stopped at that hour. Correct?"

"Yes, Duchess." My voice was humble and I didn't care.

"The reason?" Katie went on. "To fix the time of death later than the actual crime. Why? So the murderer could get away and establish an alibi. And the reason for the two watches? The killer wanted to waste no time in re-setting the old man's watch and stopping it. Then too, if he had tried to jam the case at the scene of the crime he might have broken the crystal, dropped pieces of it on the floor which he would've had to gather up and put in the vest pocket. So—he prepared the other watch first, taking no chances. He struck the old man down, beat the life out of him, changed the watches and got out of there in a hurry."

Spike nodded slowly. "And my pal, the burglar, bumped into this guy on the street, before he had a chance to get rid of the watch, and hoisted it off him."

"Or," Katie said quickly, "your pal, the burglar, is the murderer of Al Rosenblatt."

"Huh?" Spike gulped. "Naw. He's a pretty good egg, that burglar. He wouldn't kill anybody."

"Besides," I said, "the times are wrong. What time did Jake say the burglar was released? Around 2:45, wasn't it?"

"Yeah."

"Well, that let's him out," I said. "If he'd pulled the job, he'd have stopped that other watch before 2:45. So he's in the clear."

Spike sighed his relief. I think he really liked that burglar; Spike always was one to admire a man with nerve.

"He isn't in the clear," Katie promptly contradicted. "Check up and you'll probably find he has an ironclad alibi. Without a doubt he was in the office of his lawyer at three o'clock and has his lawyer and the lawyer's eight partners to swear to it."

"Wait a minute! Wait—a—minute!" I exclaimed. "Do you suppose, by any chance, your burglar's lawyer is—"

"Newman Rosenblatt!" Spike cried.

The shock of that possibility stopped us for a minute. Katie—and you have to admire her calm—was the first to speak.

"Let's stop supposing for a minute or two. Let's put our feet on the ground and get back to facts."

"Such as?" Spike asked.

"Whoever conceived this crime knew the make, the model, the initials and the type of engraving on Rosenblatt's watch. Furthermore, whoever actually pulled the job must have been a diamond buyer and must have been known by Rosenblatt. Otherwise the old man would never have opened his safe."

"That's an angle," Spike cried happily. "My burglar, by no stretch of the imagination, could ever have been a diamond buyer. He's been a burglar all his life, with maybe an occasional flier at pocket-picking."

"That's logical," I agreed. "Rosenblatt would never have opened his safe for Dopey, so we've got to come back to our original supposition. Dopey lifted the watch off the killer who, we agree, must have been known to Rosenblatt and must have been familiar with Rosenblatt's watch. And that person is—"

"Frank Leopold!" Spike and the Duchess cried in unison.

"It's a good bet," I nodded. "I happen to know that Leopold is on his last legs financially. We carried a story the other day that some of his creditors had filed an action in bankruptcy. Furthermore, we know that Rosenblatt and Leopold had trouble a couple of years ago. There's an additional motive."

"What more do we want?" Spike said.

"Oh, not much. Just enough evidence to send him to the gallows."

Katie asked: "Isn't that Captain Wallis's job? When we tell him about this watch—"

"Listen, Duchess!" Spike snorted. "Who the hell does this watch belong to?"

"It belongs, unquestionably, to the estate of Al Rosenblatt."

"Wrong as usual! It belongs, infant, to the estate of Spike Kaylor, not yet deceased. And as long as it belongs to me the police aren't going to hear anything about it. Do you gather that, Duchess, or shall I draw a diagram?"

"You're going to run it down alone?"

"You're getting positively brilliant in your deductions," Spike applauded. "We're going to run it down alone because if we gave it to Wallis he'd probably break the story for the afternoon papers—after we did all the brain work."

"We?" the Duchess asked.

"Well, I'll admit you spotted the ticker in the first place. And for that minor assistance we'll keep you in the corporation."

"Thanks. And where do we go from here?"

My partner in crime looked dubious, but I said quickly: "We send Spike to the dicks' bureau to get the number of the other watch. We wire the number to the manufacturer and find out what jeweler bought the ticker in the first place. Then we go to him and find out who he sold it to. And then—"

"We put the finger on the killer of Al Rosenblatt," Spike put in triumphantly. "Oke, Pinky?"

"Correct. How's it sound, Duchess? Simple, huh?"

"It sounds," Katie said thoughtfully, "too damned simple."

Well, it did sound that way. But the more we talked it over the more we convinced ourselves we were on the right track. Some one known to Rosenblatt bought that watch, had it engraved to match the diamond merchant's, killed the old man and planted it in his vest pocket. And then, before the killer got rid of the ticker he'd taken from Rosenblatt, Dopey McClain bumped into him on a crowded street and hoisted it.

There it was, take it or leave it. We decided to take it. We decided we were a cinch for a beautiful news beat. And we couldn't help wondering, during the following twenty-two hours, who we'd eventually put the finger on. Frank Leopold? Newman Rosenblatt? Or possibly Dopey McClain?

THE FOLLOWING DAY was a long one, because we didn't get an answer to our telegram until four in the afternoon. And when it came, and Katie and Spike and I went into a huddle down the corridor, it was pretty disappointing. It read:

Watch sold Catalina Jewelry Company Los Angeles California.

And Los Angeles was five hundred miles away!

"This," Spike groaned, "is getting more tougher fast."

"We could wire the Catalina Jewelry Company and find out—" Katie checked herself. "No," she said after a moment, "that wouldn't work. The man who bought it gave an assumed name with the initials A.Z.R. And it's ten to one the clerk in a big establishment wouldn't remember him. Boys, I'm afraid we're sunk."

"Sunk, hell!" Spike rejoined. "It'll take more'n a knockdown like this to stop us. Go back in your corner and sniff ammonia."

"It's becoming apparent, too," I remarked, "that we're

dealing with a pretty smart egg. He didn't risk buying the watch here. The jeweler might remember engraving those initials, or the watch might be traced. So he goes down to L.A. and buys it from the biggest store in the city. Yes, Spike, this is getting more tougher fast."

"But we aren't sunk. Damned if we're sunk!" Spike cried. "Only—uh—"

"Yes, yes. Go on."

"You go on, Pink."

I didn't know which way to go. "Suppose we pass the buck to Katie. How about it, Duchess?"

"I say take the watch to Captain Wallis and let him—"

"And I say nuts!" Spike snapped. "Look here! We got one card left, and maybe it's an ace in the hole. My pal, the burglar."

"Dopey? What could he do?"

"Now listen! It's an eight to five shot that Frank Leopold pulled the job. We'll get his picture—he uses a cut of his homely map in every ad he runs—and see if Dopey can identify him as the guy whose watch he hoisted. How's that?"

"It's lousy," I said.

Katie asked: "Do you think this burglar would be screwy enough to admit he hoisted a watch?"

"Well," Spike said reflectively, "he's pretty screwy."

"But hardly that screwy," I said.

"Well, you can't rule out a guy for trying. Let's get hold of Dopey and turn on the heat."

"How'll you get hold of him?"

"Jake Morris."

"Yeah? You didn't get to first base when you tried that yesterday."

"We'll get to first base today. We'll turn the heat on Jake."

"You think you can?"

"Listen, lug! I got enough on that chiseler to put him away for twenty years. He knows it, too. Remember the Phelps case?"

Yes, I remembered the Phelps case, and I knew Jake had been mixed up in it. But I doubted if Spike had anything on him. However, Jake was plenty yellow; he bluffed easily and perhaps Spike could slip over a fast one on him. It was our only bet, anyway.

"All right," I said. "Let's go over and put the bee on Jake. Duchess, you stay here. This may get rough."

"The rougher the better," Katie said promptly.

"You still don't trust us, huh?"

"Just as far, darling, as I can see you. Let's go."

We clipped a picture of Frank Leopold from an ad he'd run in Sunday's paper and ankled over to Jake's office, which was on the fourth floor of a building across the street from the Hall. The big bail bond broker was alone, his feet on his desk, a cigar in his mouth, when we walked in without the ceremony of knocking. He looked surprised and not too happy to see us.

"Hello, boys—and Miss Blayne. What you want?"

"Dopey McClain," Spike told him.

"What you want with Dopey? Ain't you got that overcoat yet? Well, if you ain't, it's your own fault. You should never shoot crap in a jail, Spike, and you should never trust a burglar."

"I got the overcoat, Jake. We want to see Dopey on another matter."

Jake grunted. "Sure. I know. You got somethin' up your sleeve, all right, else why the delegation? And when you get through with Dopey, he'll maybe get cold dogs and skip his bail. Yeah. An' won't that be nice on me. Yeah."

"Where you got him filed away?" Spike demanded.

Jake shrugged, said heavily: "I ain't puttin' out nothin'."

"Oh, no?" Spike was getting mean, and when Spike gets mean he makes an angry police dog look like a sick Pekingese. "All right, big boy. If you don't put out, I put out. And when I put out anything it'll be about Bill Phelps and that paving contract." Spike paused a moment to let that sink in. "Take it or leave it, you cheap yellow-faced, yellow-livered crook."

When you consider that Jake Morris would make two of Spike Kaylor, they were harsh words. But Jake, all at once, didn't look so big. He didn't like the reference to Bill Phelps and the paving contract. He didn't like it even a little bit.

"Can't you tell me what you want with Dopey?" he asked. "Maybe I—"

"Maybe you can go open an oyster! Where you got Dopey holed up?"

Jake took a deep breath. "You want I should call him up here?"

"You're certainly getting good at riddles, Jake. You got the answer right away."

Sighing heavily, Jake took up the telephone and called a number. He asked for McClain, got him and told him to come to his office at once. The rest of us sighed too, with relief, and sat down. We were over the first hump.

Dopey McClain showed in about ten minutes. He came in whistling cheerfully. His song died when he saw Spike.

"Well! My pal. How are you, pal? How's the newspaper racket?"

"Take a chair, Dopey."

"Sure, pal," Dopey said pleasantly. "Where'll I take it?"

"Cut it, guy! Save your comedy for the courtroom. Where'd you get that watch?"

"Watch?" Dopey sat down, not happily.

"Ticker to you, Dopey. Where'd you hoist it?"

"So help me, pal, I don't know the beef."

"You'll know it, Dopey, if I turn you in to the cops," Spike said significantly. "Haven't you been told it's a felony in this state to pick pockets?"

Dopey tried to square his shoulders as he indignantly retorted: "Pal, I'm a burglar. I ain't no dip."

"Says you!"

Spike whipped the watch out of his pocket, hopped across the room, held it in front of Dopey's face.

"Ever see this before?"

"No. I never seen it before," Dopey vowed.

"And I suppose you'll deny, when we get you on the witness stand, that it wasn't in the pocket of that overcoat I stripped off you last night?"

"If it was in there, pal. I don't know how it got there."

Spike put the watch away and took out the picture of Frank Leopold. "Ever see this guy before?" he demanded.

Dopey scanned the picture. He tweaked his long nose, scratched his head. "Well, maybe yes, maybe no. He does look kind of familiar."

"Is this the guy you hoisted the watch from?" Spike cried.

I held my breath. If Dopey said yes, well—we were plenty hot on the trail. But Dopey must have had training as a congressman. He couldn't bring himself to say either yes or no. He hemmed and hawed for a minute or two, while Spike and I sweat, and Katie perspired.

Then he pleaded: "Listen, pal! Gimme the lay, will you? You can't expect me to admit—"

"Dopey, get this!" Spike ordered ominously. "You're on the spot, guy, and it's a plenty tough spot. Prowling houses and picking pockets is one thing. Murder, Dopey, murder—is something else again. The guy you stole this watch from killed that old diamond merchant, Rosenblatt. You probably saw it in the papers."

Dopey gulped. He tweaked his nose furiously and the sweat began to roll down his pale cheeks.

"Unless," Spike barked, "you killed him!"

SPIKE WAITED A moment. The room was so tense something had to snap. And it was Dopey who snapped. Shaking like a leaf in a wind, he rasped:

"I never killed nobody! I swear I never, Spike! I hoisted that ticker off Jake Morris while we was standing in the desk sergeant's office!"

Well, it knocked the wind out of us. Spike, because he was standing, looked harder hit than anybody else. He was limp, all at once, as he swung around toward Jake Morris.

Jake's yellow teeth were clamped over his cigar. He was gripping the corner of his desk with one soiled paw. The other was thrust deep in his pocket. His face was green and his small ice-blue eyes glared viciously at Dopey.

And all at once I knew that Dopey had told the truth. I stood up.

"You should have ditched that watch sooner, Jake," I said quietly. "Though of course you thought you were safe. You had a neat alibi, very neat. At three o'clock you were in the press room, and you had all of us fellows to back you up. You figured you'd pulled the perfect job. And it would have been perfect, I guess, if you'd known that Dopey was a dip as well as a dinger. Did I hear you tell Spike, a minute ago, never to trust a burglar?"

"Pinky, you're nuts," Jake said unsteadily. "Me, I don't know what you're talkin' about."

"Like hell you don't! I suppose you went to Los Angeles two weeks ago to see the races."

"Sure I did."

"And I suppose you didn't buy a watch from the Catalina Jewelry Company? And have it engraved with the initials A.Z.R.? No, no, not you. It was a couple of other guys. It's too bad, Jake, you didn't have brains enough to file the number off that watch. But then I guess you were afraid to do that—it would have looked too suspicious. Anyway, Jake, the salesman who sold it to you is on his way up here to identify you. And you're going to have one hell of a lot of explaining to do to Captain Wells. Now do you want to come over with us and start in on it?"

WELL, I NEVER thought he'd do it. I never thought he had the guts. But all at once there it was—a big .45 automatic in Jake's shaking hand.

I took a step backward, and so did Spike. I didn't like it, not any. A frightened man is liable to do most anything, if he's scared badly enough. And Jake Morris was scared.

Scared, but not so dumb. He was thinking just as fast as we were, and maybe a shade faster. Without a word, without any other threat than the waving .45, he reached back with his left hand and found the telephone. He took a couple of steps toward us—and we took a couple of steps backward—and then he yanked the phone out by the roots.

"I oughta kill you," Jake rasped, "only it'd make too much noise. You guys are gonna stay here—locked in, see? And I'm lamming. By the time you get outta here I'll be in the clear"—and he added leering at us—"with a hundred grand in ice."

I got a glimpse of Katie out of the corner of my eye. She hadn't moved from her chair. I could see her face was dead white and I knew she was frightened. I was sorry, now, I'd let her come. Because—well, I had a hunch Spike wasn't going to take this lying down and I knew damned well I wasn't.

I managed, without being too obvious, to give Spike one quick look. I knew he'd get it. We'd worked together before. I knew that when the time came, he'd be right there with me and he'd be there low.

Jake backed toward the door. He was facing us; Katie was out of his line of vision.

"Do you want our hands up, Jake?" I asked cheerfully.

"You keep your hands where they are."

"All right, Jake. Just so you don't get nervous with that rod." I glanced at Katie, dropped my jaw, gasped: "Katie! For God's sake!"

Well, it was old stuff but show me the man who, under the circumstances, wouldn't shift his eyes an instant. And that instant was all we needed.

Spike went in low. His driving shoulder buried itself a foot deep in Jake's belly just as I made a wild leap, knocked the rod aside with my left hand and risked everything on finding Jake's button with my right. I was lucky; I had to be lucky.

The .45 went off with a roar like a twelve-inch howitzer. Pain, like a red-hot knife, shot through my fist and up my arm to the shoulder. It wasn't the bullet. It was the shock of connecting with Jake's jaw.

The big broker went down with a crash, and Spike and I landed on top of him. He was out but we took no chances. While I hastily collared the automatic, Spike gave him these and those. And when Spike finished and we stumbled to our feet. Jake Morris was slumbering peacefully but not prettily.

We both turned to Katie. She hadn't moved and her face was putty-white. But she smiled and managed in a quavering voice that was not at all like her own:

"You—you scared the hell out of me, you two."

"Huh!" Dopey McClain grunted. "If you was scared—what do you think I was? Holy cats! Never again do I hoist a ticker—not even from my best friend."

In no time at all we got the dicks over, gave them a tabloid version of the story and streaked for the press room. It was then eight minutes of six and we had just eight minutes to make our first editions. As Katie, still putty-white, started toward a phone booth she faltered. She caught hold of a chair and eased into it. She looked green around the gills and terribly frightened.

"Pinky!" she whispered. "I'm—going—to faint."

Which she proceeded to do forthwith.

We picked her up and laid her out on a desk and looked at each other.

"The excitement," Spike grinned, "was too much for Katie. Well, she'll snap out of it. In the meantime—I got about five minutes to make the bulldog with our story."

"What about the *Sun?*"

Spike glanced at the Duchess, shrugged. "To hell with the *Sun!* And to hell with the Lady and Katie! Maybe this'll teach 'em a police beat is no place for a dame. Guys, now—we don't faint. If Katie doesn't come to in time to make her first edition with the story—well, that's just too bad. She can make her second."

I decided I could be just as hard-boiled as Spike.

"Oke!" I said. "To hell with the *Sun,* and the Lady, and Katie!"

Spike went into a booth and closed the door. I got some water and threw it on the Duchess and opened the collar of her blouse.

It was certainly a rotten break for the kid. Here she'd seen it through right up to the end—and then had to go pull a stunt like this. I looked over my shoulder at Spike. I could see him, through the glass door, talking a mile a minute. I glanced back at Katie.... Oh, to hell with Spike!

I leaped into a booth and called the *Sun* and asked for the desk. The Lady came on with a terse:

"City desk! Commence!"

"This is Pinky Kane, Miss Tobin. I want to give you the end of that Rosenblatt story. Jake Morris, the bail bond broker and one-time partner of Rosenblatt, has been—"

"Moses on a bicycle," the Lady bellowed. "What is this, Kane? Be Kind to Animals Week? Spike Taylor just gave me the story."

Well, we came out of our respective booths, Spike and I,

at the same instance. We met each others' eyes, and Spike looked plenty sheepish and I know I looked the same. Spike said tentatively:

"Oh, well. She's a pretty swell little kid, anyway."

Katie, blinking, was sitting up on the desk. "Who—who are you talking about?" she asked dazedly.

"Not you, yuh mugg!" Spike retorted furiously. "Go back to sleep!"

THE DUCHESS RIDES A HUNCH

*Katie Blayne, Known to the Press-Room
Gang as the Duchess, Had a Hunch Which
Moved Her to the Head of the Killer's List*

1

WHEN HE CALLED out: "Look, Duchess!" I realized that Jeff Gervin, of the *Sentinel,* had had a few drinks. Jeff is mean when he's drinking. He has to rib somebody, and the season is never closed on Katie Blayne, who covers the police beat for the *Sun.*

"Look, Duchess!" Jeff spoke out of the side of his mouth, squinting at Katie, one bushy eyebrow higher than the other. "You got a home, Duchess? Some place—any place—you got a home and family?"

Katie Blayne, slim and blond and lovely, strolled placidly to the press-room window and stood looking out on the street.

"Because if you got a home, Duchess," Jeff went on, "why aren't you in it? It's your day off, isn't it? Why the postman's holiday?"

Pete Zerker, of the *Bulletin,* picked up a telephone and started to call the beat: northern, eastern, fire alarm, the two emergencies, the morgue. Spike Kaylor, day police reporter for my paper, the *Bulletin,* continued a desultory game of solitaire.

After a while the door opened and Rosenberg, a handsome six feet and a hard two hundred pounds of shyster lawyer, came into the room. He nodded to us, smiled at Katie and greeted her with: "How's it, baby?"

The Duchess turned on her charm. "Hello, Rosie. How are you?"

"I'm great," the beefy shyster beamed. "Sorry I kept you waiting. Look. I've got a phone call to make, then I'll be right with you."

Rosie went out. The Duchess produced a compact and started making up her lips.

"Baby!" I said, and I guess my voice was pretty bitter. "When did you start playing around with that ton of shyster?"

"Rosie? Why, Rosie and I have been pals for years," Katie said brightly. "Do you mind?"

Well, it wasn't any place for an argument, even if I'd had a good one. I walked over to Jeff's desk and helped myself to a drink. After a minute or two Rosie threw open the door again.

"All right, baby," he beamed. "Let's scram."

I watched them go out, as handsome a pair as you'd see in a day's walk along Hollywood Boulevard. Jeff Gervin started to say something, but I didn't give him a chance.

"Look, you muggs!" I said. "Have any of you got a smart crack to make about Katie Blayne?... Or Rosie?... Or me?"

No one, it appeared, had any cracks to make.

I helped myself to another shot of Jeff's liquor, found a copy of the *Bulletin's* last edition and took a chair for myself. I heard Jeff whisper to Pete Zerker something about "can't stand competition. Rosie sure is a handsome shyster, huh?"

I kept busy with the *Bulletin*. After all, I'd laid myself open. I ought to be able to take it if the gang felt like dishing it.

*"Take it easy, kid. We're
in a tough spot"*

In less than an hour Katie Blayne, looking strangely white, was back in the press room.

"Hi, Duchess!" Jeff hailed. "Where's your handsome ton o' shyster?"

Katie walked abstractedly to her desk and sat down. She picked up her telephone, hesitated, put it back on the desk. She sat staring at the opposite wall, without seeing it. There was horror and hurt in her fine blue eyes.

"Katie!" I said. "What's wrong?"

"Did the naughty shyster get fresh with our sweet-sy-weetsy baby?" Jeff Gervin croaked.

We didn't pay any attention to him. I walked over and put my hand on Katie's shoulder. She looked up at me and I was shocked to see her eyes were glistening. It takes something, it takes a lot, to bring tears to the eyes of our hard little Duchess.

"Please, Pinky," she said quietly.

Well, that was that. I picked up my paper. Spike resumed his solitaire and Pete started to call the beat again. From force of habit I listened to him, heard him say at last:

"Hello, morgue. Zerker of the *Bulletin*. Anything?"

And right there I felt my skin begin to prickle.

"Yes?" Pete Zerker said. "Oh, yes… Yes, I have it… I see… Heart failure, you say? Well, he was the type… Office of J. G. Gross and Company?… Dead when the ambulance got there?… O.K., Coroner. Thank you."

Pete hung up. He looked around the room, but his eyes avoided Katie Blayne.

"Rosie Rosenberg," he said quietly, "is dead."

WELL, WE'D KNOWN it. We'd sensed it as Pete was talking to the coroner. And yet the feeling of shock was heavy in the room. Somehow it didn't seem possible. Big, healthy, handsome Rosie—dead! Packed off to the morgue in the meat wagon like a common floater fished out of the bay.

Yes, somehow it didn't seem possible. And yet there it was. And there was Katie, looking stunned and hurt and, strangely, just a bit vindictive.

Jeff Gervin said heavily: "Well, he was a right guy at that. Anybody want a game of rummy?"

Nobody wanted a game of rummy.

There was a brief silence. Then, abruptly, Katie was on her feet.

"It's phony!" she cried. "Rosie didn't drop dead of heart failure. Rosie—darn it! Rosie was *murdered!*"

I went over and put my arm around her. "Take it easy, kid. Sit down and take it easy. Do you want to tell us about it?"

She shrugged out of my arm and sat down again. I went

back to my chair across the room. She had hold of herself now; she spoke in the detached manner of a reporter phoning in a story.

"Rosie and I went up to see J.B. Gross, who's in the oil lease racket and has offices in the Sheldon Building. You probably know him. A thin, sickly, middle-aged bag of bones."

"We know the crook," I said. "Go on, kid."

"Gross has about a dozen stenographers in his main office. His private office is separated from this big room by a glass partition. Gross sits in there and keeps his eagle eye on everybody."

"He's the type," Spike Kaylor growled.

"I waited in the outer office with the stenos," Katie went on. "Rosie went in to see Gross. They talked for fifteen or twenty minutes. Gross sat like a wax figure in a museum. He never moved. He said hardly a word. Rosie got mad, I guess, because he started striding up and down, talking like a whirlwind and waving his arms."

"Rosie always was excitable," Pete Zerker commented.

"Anyway, all of a sudden Rosie stopped talking. He put both hands up to his throat and collapsed. I ran into the room, along with three or four of the stenos. Gross, even then, didn't get out of his chair. He said:

" 'Rosenberg has a very bad heart. Just open the windows, girls. A little fresh air will bring him around. He shouldn't excite himself, with a heart like that.'

"We opened all the windows and let in the cold air. Rosie didn't come around. He looked ghastly and finally I made Gross phone for an ambulance. The interne who came with the wagon said Rosie was dead. Heart failure, he called it.

So they carted him off to the morgue… and I came back here"—her voice rose in bitter anger—*"and Rosie didn't die of heart failure!"*

She was pretty close to hysteria by that time and we, even Jeff Gervin, had sense enough not to question her for a while. Finally, when she seemed clear, I asked her what she and Rosie were doing in the office of J.B. Gross.

"The *Sun*," Katie told us, "is working up an exposé of the oil lease racket. Rosie used to be Gross's attorney. He knew all the ins and outs of the game. Gross owed him money, about eight thousand dollars. Rosie went up there today to tell Gross that unless he paid up he'd spill all he knew. He's been putting the bee on Gross every few days for months."

"There's your motive," I said. "If Rosie ever spilled the works, J.B. Gross would draw a stretch on McNeil's Island."

"Yeah, there's a motive," Spike Kaylor agreed. "But what other reason have you got for thinking Rosie was rubbed out? And how was the job pulled?"

Well, that slowed her down to a walk. It practically stopped her.

"*Other* reason!" Jeff Gervin sneered. "She hasn't given any reason yet."

"Only a motive," Zerker commented.

Well, I saw we wouldn't get anywhere with those three skeptics. I took Katie's arm and went out of the room. We strolled up and down the corridor and talked things over.

Now, although Katie and I cover police for rival morning papers, we occasionally work together. Our offices, of course, know nothing of this cooperation. City editors don't consider it cricket, or something, for their reporters to work with men from a rival sheet.

Now Katie had a hunch. The rest of the gang might laugh at her—had laughed at her many times in the past, to their sorrow—but I'd string along. I know Katie, and I know Katie's hunches…

2

BUT FIRST, JUST to get away from the emotion and senti-
ment, I tried to talk her out of it. I pointed out it was a
well-known fact that Rosie had a very weak heart. Hadn't
he stopped drinking four years ago because the doctors
told him a few shots of liquor would knock him for a loop?

"You see, Katie, it was the logical way for an excitable
man like Rosie to die."

"And do you think J.B. Gross didn't know that? And
count on the fact that everybody who knew Rosie knew
he had a bad heart and might drop off any time?"

"That's perfectly true," I admitted. "On the other hand,
if Gross murdered him, don't you think the autopsy will
show he did it?"

"And do you think," Katie demanded scornfully, "that
Gross would be stupid enough to kill him by some method
that a nitwit autopsy surgeon would bring to light?"

"Well, what do you want to do about it? Tell your story
to Captain Wallis and let him check on it?"

It was a dumb question. There's nothing the Duchess
enjoys more than puzzling out a mystery without benefit
of the police department.

"I take it then, Pinky, that you want none of it."

"Then you have me wrong. Katie, I want it all. Every bit
of it, for you and me. Tell me what you want to do."

"I want to go up to Gross's office tonight, break into it if we have to, and search it from truck to keelson. Are you with me?"

"Count me in. It's burglary, kid, but do we give a hoot? I have the late shift tonight and I won't be off till two. Meet me on the corner of Eighth and Broadway at two-ten tomorrow morning.

The Sheldon Building, where Gross had his offices, should have been condemned thirty years ago. It had no night watchman, no central heating, no elevator, and very few tenants. However, all that was all right with us.

Katie got into Gross's office on the third floor via my shoulders and the transom. Except for a panicky half minute when she was stuck in the transom and I thought we might have to call the fire department to get her out, it was a cinch. She opened the door for me and I joined her in the musty-smelling office springing the latch behind me.

Switching on my flashlight, I let Katie guide me through the chill gloom of the main office to Gross's private room. The door was unlocked and we went in. I shot the light around the room, careful not to let it strike a window.

It was a small office and there wasn't much in it. Gross's ancient flat-topped desk; two chairs; a circulating room heater, painted in imitation of walnut; a green, single-tier filing cabinet; a water cooler with an inverted five-gallon jug of water.

"Not much here that a man could use to commit murder," I remarked.

"Did you expect to find a machine gun mounted on the desk?" Katie acidly retorted.

We went over the room and its furnishings with a fine-tooth comb. And at the end of an hour we admitted we were licked.

"Any use to try the main office?" I asked.

"No. Whatever he used, if he used anything, would be in here. I was in the outer office when Rosie passed out and the door between the two rooms was shut."

"Then I guess we'd better call it a night."

"I suppose so, Pinky." The Duchess sighed; she was one disheartened little girl. "And I was so sure—so *sure* we'd find a clue. See here! You don't think I'm being foolish, do you? Riding a hunch so hard? Dragging you into committing a felony?"

"Skip the felony, kid. You can't be a felon till you're caught."

"But, Pinky! Do you think I'm foolish?"

I never answered her. At that instant she jerked the flash out of my hand and switched it off.

"Listen!" she hissed.

I listened, and what I heard wasn't good news. A key was rattling in the door of the outer office. A moment later the rusty hinges creaked and a beam of light, nothing more that we could see, came barging into the big room.

I PULLED KATIE against me. "Take it easy, kid. We're in a tough spot, but we've been in other tough spots together. Just sit tight and let me handle this."

The light was advancing down the aisle between the desks and I could tell that the person who carried it knew his way around the office. When he was a dozen feet from the door of the inner room I could make out a lanky angular body behind the flash.

J.B. Gross in person! J.B. Gross stealthily entering his

own office in the middle of the night, afraid to switch on the lights!

Gross had stopped short about three paces from the doorway to his private office. And I realized what stopped him. He'd left the door closed and now he found it open.

I heard my heart pounding as I caught Katie by the arm and, just in time, jerked her down below the wooden part of the wall. Gross's light swept the inner office, over our heads. Katie swayed against me and I felt her tremble.

"Don't worry, kid," I whispered. "I'll take him like Grant took Richmond!"

"B-b-b-but, Pinky! He prob'ly has a gun!"

I hadn't thought of that particular angle. And thinking about it, in the three or four seconds I had in which to do my thinking, I didn't like it. Not any.

"Stay right here!" I whispered "Flat on the floor."

Her fingers closed tight on my arm for an instant, and then I moved toward the door on all fours. Just inside the casing I waited, crouched and ready for Mr. J.B. Gross. Of course if Mr. J.B. Gross was ready for me—well, that would be too bad for somebody and the somebody was a cinch to be Pinky Kane.

Gross's light stopped swinging and centered on the doorway. It came closer and just as it moved into the room I hopped to my feet, dragging a right from my shoe tops.

The light behind the flash was dim, but not too dim. I made out Gross's bony head and let him have it right behind the ear. The light went out and Gross went down without a murmur.

I got my own flash from Katie and switched it on. Gross looked like a sack of bones lying on the floor. He was out cold. Beside him lay a long cylindrical package wrapped in a newspaper. I caught it up under my arm and we got out of there in a hurry.

We didn't slow down until we were in my car and a dozen blocks from the Sheldon Building. Then I pulled up under a street light and shut off the motor.

"Well, Katie, what do you think we drew in the grab bag?"

"Something," Katie said confidently, "that will explain how Rosie was murdered this afternoon."

I unrolled the newspaper and brought to light—a section of three-inch stove pipe. Nothing more. Just a section of cheap stovepipe you could buy in any hardware store for fifteen cents. I looked at the Duchess and the Duchess looked somewhere else.

"Now what the hell!" I grumbled. "Does this length of pipe mean anything to you?"

"Not a thing," Katie said unhappily.

"And yet," I said, "here's a guy sneaking it into his own office in the dead of night. What's the answer?"

"The answer is that Gross murdered Rosie Rosenberg and this piece of pipe would explain how he did it. If we were bright enough to figure it out!"

"Yes, if we were bright enough to figure it out," I repeated unhappily. "Well, shall we give up and—"

"And take the pipe to Captain Wallis? Not any! We'll sleep over this, Pinky. And we'll work it out, you and I alone, together."

I got down to the press room about noon the next day. Katie was already on the job, calling the beat like a veteran, while the three other police reporters played rummy.

I sat down on the edge of her desk. "Any ideas, kid?"

She smiled and shook her head. "You?"

"A darb."

I nodded toward the door and Katie followed me out into the corridor. I turned to her and said:

"Duchess, I got a hunch. It's a pip. I'm going over to the library to check something. Then you and I are hopping up to Gross's office. Of course he won't talk, unless he tells us what a terrible heart Rosie had. But there's something there I want to see. And if I find what I think I'll find—kid, it's the rope for J.B. Gross. Now look! You haven't tipped your office on this murder angle, have you?"

"No"

"Good! Now—"

"*Well!*"

3

THE WORD WAS like a healthy slap in the face. I turned
and there was Miss Jane Tobin, probably the one person in
the world I had no yen to see at the moment. Miss Tobin,
known to her loyal underlings as the Lady, is city editor
of the *Sun*. Don't tell me women city editors are as rare as
undivorced movie stars. I know it as well as you do. They
made one, Jane Tobin, and then broke the mold. Thank
goodness.

There she stood in all her virginal glory, slight of build,
middle-aged, dowdy, her out-moded peach-basket hat
cocked over her left ear, a smudge of printer's ink on her
nose—and fire in her steely blue eyes.

"Well!" she repeated, in a bull voice you could hear for
six blocks. "And what is it, young lady, that you haven't
tipped your office to? And what have I told you about
collaborating with these press room tramps? What have
I told you particularly about playing around with Pinky
Kane? What—well, what in Sam Hill have you got to say
for yourself?"

Katie flushed and looked at the floor. Of course, I had
to put in my oar and virtually capsize the boat.

"Be yourself, Miss Tobin," I said. "We just happened to
be working together on this story and—"

"Working together!" the Lady stormed. "I knew it! I

knew it as soon as I saw the two of you whispering. Working together, huh? Damn it, Pinky Kane, I'm going to tell you a few things about the newspaper business. And then I'm going to tell Katie a few. Yes, plenty! Look here, Kane, you gnat-brained, double-crossing—"

I never found out what she wanted to tell me. I dove into the press room and slammed the door. Ten minutes later, looking meek and chastened. Katie came in. She glanced at me, smiled wryly and not very happily.

"It's no soap, Pinky. I'm on my own from now on. Orders."

"Listen! How long are you going to let that half-witted back number tell you how to handle your beat?"

Katie's eyes flashed as she asserted staunchily: "Miss Tobin's not half-witted, Pinky Kane, and she's not a back number. She knows more about the newspaper racket in five minutes than you and your press room gang know in a year. And she's one hell of a swell boss!"

"Sock him, Duchess!" Jeff Gervin chirped.

I ignored Jeff. "Look, Duchess. What do you want me to do about this story?"

Katie shrugged. "It was mine in the first place, Pinky. I had the hunch, you know."

"Oke!" I snapped. "You can have it. And if you think you can work it out without any help from me, you'd better take another guess for yourself."

"Sure, Duchess," Jeff piped, "take two guesses. And then dust. We want to play rummy."

I got out of there and went over to the library. I was pretty sore, but not as sore as I might have been. After all, you can't condemn a girl for being loyal.

An hour later I left the library on the double, raced back to the press room and found the three rummy hounds deep in their game. No Katie.

"Where's the Duchess?" I demanded.

"Who cares?" growled Jeff Gervin.

I caught him by the nape of the neck and jerked him backwards over the chair onto his feet.

"Damn it, where's the Duchess?"

Jeff Gervin sputtered inarticulately. Spike Kaylor's jaw dropped. Pete Zerker looked me over with sharp discerning eyes. He rose slowly.

"What's wrong. Pinky?"

"Plenty! If you know where Katie is, tell me."

"Her office phoned about twenty minutes ago," Pete said tersely. "She talked to the Lady for a few minutes and then went out. We don't know where she went."

I caught up Katie's office phone and called for the city desk. The Lady came on with a crisp:

"Miss Tobin speaking. Commence!"

"This is Pinky Kane, Lady. Where's Katie?" I heard her gasp, but I didn't give her a chance to sound off. "Listen! If you've sent that girl to Gross's office you've probably signed her death warrant. Do you get that? Now where is she?"

"She's at Gross's," the Lady shot back. "Get over there in a hurry, Kane. I'll be with you."

As snappy as that. No hows or whys, no wasting time with stupid questions. That's the Lady.

I tossed the phone aside and leaped for the door.

WINDED LIKE A quarter-miler at the end of a tough race, I reached the third floor of the Sheldon Building and tumbled into Gross's office. A dozen typewriters stopped rattling and a dozen startled faces turned toward mine.

Across the room on the other side of the glass partition I saw Katie Blayne and J.B. Gross. The oil lease racketeer was behind his desk. With his angular and hairless head, his dead-white sunken cheeks, his deep-set bright black eyes, he looked like an incarnation of the devil.

Katie sat facing him. Even through the glass, from a distance of forty feet, she looked pale and sick. Talk about arriving in the nick of time!

I raced across the room and through the flimsy door to the inner office without even stopping to turn the knob. Katie heard me coming and swung around in her chair. As I crashed through the door she stood up. And that exertion, slight as it was, got her.

She swayed. She tried to say something and couldn't. I caught her in the crook of my left arm. I grabbed her chair and swung it with a looping motion over my head and through the outer window, conscious all the time of that sinister, motionless death's head across the desk.

Picking up the Duchess, I carried her to the smashed window and as the fresh cold air beat in on her face she stirred. My own head began to reel and I put her on her feet. I took a couple of gulps of air and looked around for J.B. Gross.

He was moving stealthily, with a dead minimum of effort, toward the circulating room heater which stood against the wall midway between his desk and the door. He was watching me with those awful sunken black eyes which never seemed to blink.

Well, it was sheer insanity to do it, to move, to breathe

that air. It was sheer insanity, panting as I was, to get away from the window.

But there was something driving me. With my head reeling, warning caution, I forgot caution and leaped toward J.B. Gross. He retreated to the far corner of the room. He didn't jump, or run. He glided backwards, smoothly and effortlessly, his unblinking black eyes fixed on me with a deadly intensity.

I didn't dare trust my fist. I was too groggy. I couldn't see clearly and my reflexes were all jumped up. I picked up the other chair and raised it over my head.

As I lurched toward Gross he slid down in the corner in a formless heap. He looked just as I'd seen him last, like a bundle of bones in a wrinkled black broadcloth sack. He raised his bloodless talon hands and locked them over his hairless skull. He croaked: "Don't hit me! Please don't hit me, mister!"

I hated to do it, but not very much. I brought the chair down crashing on his head. And then went out like a light.

When I came to, the back of my neck was resting on the window sill. Katie and half a dozen stenographers were holding me there, with my head out in the cold air. I took a few deep breaths and knew I was coming around O.K.

"I don't know the score, Pinky," the Duchess said. "But I knew you had to have fresh air."

"Smart girl! You all right?"

"Yes. A little shaky still, but getting better fast."

The stenos were babbling questions, two or three of them half hysterical. In the far corner lay J.B. Gross. A couple of girls were bending over him, wiping away the blood that oozed from a deep gash across the top of his bald head.

I shooed them away. "Let him alone. If the dirty rat dies, it'll save the state the expense of hanging him."

They tried to argue with me, but I wasn't in the mood and I finally ran the whole gang out of the room. Then, still a bit groggy, I staggered over to the gas heater, which was going full blast, and turned it off. By this time, with all the windows open, the office was full of cold fresh air.

Katie came over. "What was it, Pinky? Carbon monoxide?"

"Right. I'll show you."

I pointed to the vent which led from the heater into the wall. It was ordinary three-inch pipe. But midway in the single section there was a damper. And the damper was closed!

"You see, these gas heaters give off carbon monoxide when they're going full tilt. That's the reason for the vent, to carry it off. But that vent is never, under any circumstances, fitted with a damper when it's installed."

"Of course not. If you close the vent the carbon monoxide will escape into the room."

"All right. J.B. Gross was hot. He was so hot that a tip from Rosenberg to the Federal authorities would have sent him over for a long stretch. Rosie was threatening him and he decided to rub Rosie out.

"So he bought a section of three-inch pipe with a damper in it. He substituted it for the section the stove was fitted with and what'd he have?"

"A neat little lethal chamber," the Duchess said promptly.

"Exactly. Yesterday when Rosie came in he flipped that

damper and started sending the carbon monoxide into the room. And Rosie died— Today—"

"I get it," Katie said breathlessly. "He talked to me for a while and I gave him the works. I told him I was working on my own. I let him think I was all by myself up here last night and conked him with a flashlight. And I hinted he might be able to buy me off. That's when he got up, saying the room felt cold, and went over and adjusted the heater."

"You mean, that's when he decided to put you to sleep."

4

KATIE FROWNED. "HE certainly had nerve, or else he's a bit cracked. Two deaths from heart failure in this office would have looked rather suspicious."

"What of it? If he'd got rid of that section of pipe with the damper in it before the police started checking up he'd have been in the clear, wouldn't he? Even though they found the heater's vent pipe was missing, Gross could plead ignorance, couldn't he?"

"And that section of pipe we picked up last night—" Katie began.

"Was the section he'd removed. He was sneaking up here to put it back and get rid of the one with the damper. When we ran off with it he had to let it wait a day. He couldn't buy another this morning and come up here and install it in front of the stenographers."

The Duchess nodded thoughtfully. "But—but, Pinky!" she cried abruptly. "Gross was in the room all the time himself, breathing those deadly fumes. If Rosie died, and you and I passed out, why did he suffer no ill effects?"

"Ah! There you have the cleverest angle of the whole plot. You see, Gross—"

At that instant a bull voice cried hoarsely from the doorway: "What in Sam Hill goes on here?"

I groaned. Yes, of course. It was the Lady, breathless and

disheveled her absurd hat cocked on one ear, the inevitable smudge of ink on her chin. She strode into the room in a way that made her seem three times her size. She took hold of Katie's arms and looked at her hard. Then she whirled and confronted me.

"And you, you big palooka, told me I'd signed her death warrant," the Lady stormed. "She looks pretty much alive to me. What's the bright idea, scaring me half to death that way?"

"You tell her, Katie," I said weakly. "I've got something else on my mind."

I went over to the window and lost my lunch. Excitement and carbon monoxide, I guess, are a tough combination. I must have hung over that window for an hour, retching, and wanting to die, and afraid I wasn't going to.

I have a vague recollection of Captain Wallis showing up a few minutes after the Lady. And right on his tail Pete Zerker, and Spike Kaylor and Jeff Gervin. There was a lot of conversation, but I wasn't interested in it.

I recall hearing a couple of wagon men come in and dump J.B. Gross on a stretcher. I heard one of them say: "No fracture, apparently. He'll snap out of it."

My head cleared at last and I stopped retching. Everybody had gone by that time except Katie, Captain Wallis and Inspector Jenkins. Katie and I stayed there for quite a while, answering questions, delving into Gross's records.

When finally we shoved off, Wallis and Jenkins were still rummaging through the office. We drove around for a couple of hours; you can't get too much fresh air after a dose of carbon monoxide. When we got back to the press room it was late in the afternoon.

Pete Zerker was just hanging up the telephone as we walked in. "You called the turn, Pinky. The coroner says Rosie died of monoxide poisoning. With that bad heart of his, one good whiff was all he needed"

Spike Kaylor looked up from another phone. "The dicks have found the hardware store where Gross bought the pipe with the damper. The clerk hasn't slept since, remembering that hairless mug."

Jeff Gervin, as usual, was pouring himself a drink. "Just talked to the Emergency, Pink. Gross snapped out of it oke. We'll have the fun of going over to Quentin and watching his last waltz."

"Oh, yeah?" Spike Kaylor growled. "I'll offer even money Gross beats the rap. Why? Because the set-up doesn't make sense. Here you got Gross sitting there at his desk inhaling that stuff, watching Rosie kick off. The same when Katie passed out. And Pinky. How'd he do it? How'd he come out alive himself? I tell you it doesn't make sense. Except for that, it's an open-and-shut case. When the jury hears he sat there and took it himself, there'll be no soap."

I looked at the Duchess. "Shall I tell 'em, Katie?"

"Let 'em wait," Katie said.

THEY DIDN'T HAVE to wait long. A few minutes later, Captain Wallis walked into the press room. "Here's a page, evidently torn out of a book on chemistry," he announced. "We found it in Gross's desk. One paragraph is marked. Thought you fellows would like to know about it. I'll read it to you.

" 'The speed with which a person succumbs to carbon monoxide is governed by the victim's rate of metabolism. It is obvious, then, that a young person will succumb more quickly than an older person, a healthy person more quickly than one who is not well. Whether or not a person is exerting himself is also a vital factor. A man might sit motionless, breathing shallowly, and suffer no ill effects in the presence of sufficient gas to kill another person who was moving around and breathing faster and more deeply.'"

Captain Wallis folded the page and stowed it in his pocket. "Rosenberg was excitable. He was young. Save for a bad heart, he was in perfect health. By contrast, Gross was calm during their talk. He's past middle age. In the bargain he's been virtually a walking corpse for years. That's why, having studied the properties and effects of monoxide, he knew he was perfectly safe in using it to murder Rosenberg. He knew beyond all doubt that Rosenberg would pass out and, with his bad heart, probably die long before he himself felt any effects of the gas.

"Miss Blayne is young and healthy, too. It got her. So is Kane, and it got him faster than either Rosenberg or Miss Blayne because he'd run up two flights of stairs and was panting like a winded whippet when he rushed into the office. Not to mention his exertions when he got in there. Anyway, I think that cleans up the case. I've filed a murder charge and will present the evidence to the grand jury."

Wallis went out. And again Spike Kaylor grinned and started to beef.

"I still don't get it. Here's a guy commits a perfect crime—at least it would have been perfect if the Duchess wasn't addicted to hunches and Pinky Kane wasn't always stringing along with her. He pulls a plenty smart one, and then he balls up the detail by leaving that marked page in his desk. He must have known something might go wrong, that the cops might get suspicious, and search his office. And certainly he knew that even the dumbest kind of a copper, lamping that marked message, would tumble to the whole set-up. I tell you it doesn't make sense "

Pete Zerker nodded slowly. "You're dead right, Spike. Without that marked passage the D.A. would never get a conviction. It was the one thing Captain Wallis needed to slip the noose around Gross's skinny neck. Coupled with the purchase of the damper, and the results of the post mortem on Rosie and the attempt to kill Katie, that page from the chemistry book adds the final touch to the state's case."

"But how a smart hombre like Gross," Spike groaned, "could be so dumb as to leave that page lying around where—"

He broke off. I felt his eyes on me and I became very busy lighting a cigarette. I felt all the others' eyes on me and I got even busier lighting that cigarette. There was quite a long silence, while I blew smoke rings at the ceiling.

"Look here, Pinky Kane," Pete Zerker began at last. "Didn't you go over to the library early this afternoon?"

"Yes, Pink, and don't you know it's a misdemeanor to tear pages out of library books?" Spike Kaylor piped up.

"Yeah, mugg, and hasn't anybody wised you that it's a felony to plant evidence?" Jeff Gervin demanded.

I winked at the Duchess. "Boys, you can't be a felon 'til you're caught. So what?"

THE DUCHESS PULLS A FAST ONE

Katie Blayne's Bluff Forces a Mysterious
Insurance Murderer into the Open

1

THE THREE OF us, Spike and Katie Blayne and I, were alone in the City Hall press room. It was six thirty of a dark and rainy evening. I'd just taken over the beat from Spike, for the *Telegram*, and Katie was waiting for the *Sun's* night police reporter to come on the job.

"Duchess," Spike Kaylor beefed, "why don't you scram out of here and go home?"

"Spike, why don't you give yourself up?" the Duchess retorted, smiling.

"Pinky, doesn't she get in your hair the way she hangs around and hangs around, all the time?" Spike persisted.

I didn't say anything. I didn't want to be drawn into their quarrel which, for seven months, had kept the press room on pins and needles. In the first place, Spike Kaylor is my best friend. And in the second place, Katie Blayne—well, never mind about Katie Blayne.

The fire alarm gong tapped out 236. Spike strode over to the card tacked on the bulletin board. "Fifth and Chesnut." He looked more cheerful. "Our City Hall apparatus will roll on the deuce."

"And you, dear little boys, I suppose, will take a ride on the big old fire engine," Katie jeered. "Won't that be just ducky!"

*Bergstrom directed them
toward the closet*

"Well," I said, "it's some consolation to be able to do something that you can't do."

Katie's blue eyes twinkled. "Maybe you think I can't."

"Skip it," I said. "You're not going kiting around on any fire truck. Not the way these lunatics drive."

At that instant the second alarm clanged in. "There's the deuce!" Spike shouted, and leaped toward the door.

I was on his heels and I realized, unhappily, that Katie was on mine. We tore down the corridor and into the fire house. The big pumper was just starting to roll. The three of us caught the hand rail and swung onto the running board. Two firemen up beside the driver looked back and yelled at Katie. The roar of the powerful engines drowned their words and the Duchess looked the other way.

As the pumper turned into the street with a breath-taking skid and roared away with bell clanging and siren wailing, Katie swayed toward me and shouted happily: "I've always wanted to do this."

"It's just the little girl in you," I growled.

We saw the red glow in the sky while we were still blocks away from the fire. Huge clouds of yellow smoke were rolling upward.

"Kurt Bergstrom's chemical plant is at Fourth and Chesnut," I yelled.

"Fine!" Spike shouted. "And if Bergstrom is going up in smoke with his chemicals, I'll buy the drinks."

Which is the way most newspaper men feel about Kurt Bergstrom. The head of the Bergstrom Chemical Company is an inventor, a nationally known chemist, a man of wealth and substance. But! He'll stoop to any gag, short of murder, to get his name in the papers. And reporters do not like publicity hounds.

The pumper pulled up a block from the fire. Katie and Spike and I piled off and started down the street as one of the firemen yelled: "Hey, Duchess! Next time you want to go to a fire, hire a cab!"

"Thanks for the buggy ride," Katie called sweetly, and blew him a kiss.

THE FIRE, WE discovered with some disappointment, was confined to the north wing of the two-story brick building. It was evidently already under control, despite the billowing clouds of acrid smoke which rolled out of the shattered windows.

"Not much to this," I remarked.

Then we saw an elderly man talking excitedly to Battalion Chief Murphy. We pegged him for the night watchman and ran over.

"He was in the chem lab in the north wing when I come on at six," the old man was saying. "He was alone, workin' on some experiment. I goes over the plant and I'm down in my room makin' some coffee, when I smell smoke. That's about a half hour later. I runs upstairs and the whole chem lab is in flames. I never seen him go out. His car's right there in front of the office where he parked it, but he ain't nowheres around."

"Who?" Spike bellowed. "Who?"

The watchman blinked at us. "Mr. Hamlin. Mr. John Hamlin. He's Mr. Bergstrom's assistant in the lab."

Chief Murphy grunted. "Well, we'll find out if he's in there in a few minutes. I'll send in a couple of men with gas masks."

A little later they found the body, or what was left of it. They didn't even try to carry it out. They left that grisly job to the coroner. In the confined space of the laboratory the heat had been intense.

We cleaned up as many angles of the story as we could and then Spike called a cab. The Duchess, as usual, was right on our heels. She climbed into the taxi with us and sat down calmly between Spike and me.

Spike stared straight ahead as the cab pulled away from the curb. "My nose tells me it's still with us," he commented acidly.

"My Christmas Night perfume," Katie said blandly. "Don't you adore it?"

"I'd adore to drop you down a manhole," Spike groused.

She let that pass. "Are you by any chance going to the Hotel Drake?" she asked. "Because if you are, I'll go with you and we'll interview Kurt Bergstrom together."

Spike groaned, but didn't argue.

The clerk at the Drake directed us to the dining room and the head waiter told us Bergstrom was eating alone in the south alcove. Spike started off, then checked himself. A cagey look came into his eyes as he asked casually: "How long has Mr. Bergstrom been in the dining room?"

"Since a little after six, sir."

As we paraded through the room, a bit damp and sooty and bedraggled, Katie asked:

"Now what was the occasion for that question?"

"Did you ever hear, my little cabbage, of the crime called arson?"

"Yes," Katie said promptly, "and I've also heard of the crime called murder. But if you're thinking of them in connection with Kurt Bergstrom, you'd best forget them. Mr. Bergstrom is a wealthy man. He had no reason to stoop to arson, much less to murder."

"That mugg would stoop to anything to get his name in the papers."

BERGSTROM ROSE WHEN he saw us coming. He was a heavy-set chap of fifty, with very pink cheeks, keen blue eyes and close-clipped blond hair.

"Goot evening, gentlemen. Goot evening, Miss Blayne." He knew every reporter in the city. "There is something I can do for you?"

"There sure is," Spike said. "Who is John Hamlin?"

"Hamlin is my assistant in the laboratory."

"Not any more he isn't your assistant." Spike never beat around the bush. "The north wing of your plant was just gutted by fire. Hamlin was burned to death, or so the watchman believes. Anyway, the firemen found a body in the lab. Hamlin's car is out in front but Hamlin is missing."

Bergstrom took it calmly but that didn't prove anything. He's the type who never shows emotion.

"Now about this man Hamlin," Spike hurried on. "Was he married?"

"Yes. He lived with his wife at 17 Bay Terrace."

"Why was he down there after hours?"

"An experimental chemist," Bergstrom proclaimed, "has no hours. He was working nights on an experiment of his own. Only during the day did he help me with one of my inventions."

"Which is?"

Bergstrom brightened. "An inexpensive device for recording sound on motion picture film. An attachment for the home movie camera, selling for only a few dollars, which—"

"Give the details to the advertising department," Spike broke in. "We're not handing out any free publicity for your invention." He paused, looked the big German straight in the eye. "Do you believe, Mr. Bergstrom, that the body found was John Hamlin's?"

Bergstrom shrugged, said cautiously: "You say Hamlin iss missing und a body was found in the laboratory. Surely you, as a brilliant young newspaper man, should be able to draw the obvious conclusion."

"But perhaps," Spike said slowly, "the conclusion is too *damned* obvious!" He glared at the bristling Bergstrom. "Have you stopped to think of that?"

"I haff hardly had time," Bergstrom retorted stiffly, "to

think of anything. Und now if you excuse me please, I run oud to the plant."

We followed him out of the dining room. In the lobby Katie asked: "Are you going out to see Mrs. Hamlin?"

"Yes, *darling!*" Spike shot back. "And I suppose you'd like to tag along."

"Yes, *dear!* I'd love it. You know how I enjoy your company."

WE FOUND MRS. Hamlin dry-eyed and calm, though we knew immediately when we saw her that she had been informed of her husband's death. She was a tall, big-boned woman with black hair that looked dyed and dark, close-set eyes.

She invited us into the living room and asked us to sit down. "I knew that those experiments would end in tragedy," she told us calmly. "You see, my husband was developing a high explosive."

"So far as anyone knows," Spike pointed out, "there was no explosion."

"The chemicals he used were highly inflammable."

"I see." Spike didn't look as though he saw at all. "Did your husband come home for dinner tonight, Mrs. Hamlin?"

"He came home, yes. He ate an early dinner, as always, and rushed back to the laboratory. He must have got there a little before six. I did my dishes and sat down and tried to read. I had planned to go to a movie. But, somehow, I didn't dare leave the house. I was sitting here on the Chesterfield when the coroner phoned. I was neither surprised nor shocked. You see, I have been expecting this." She wiped her dry eyes with a folded handkerchief. "I suppose you will want pictures?"

She turned to a table, picked up three large snapshots and handed them to me. "They were taken a year ago today. Our wedding day."

Well, it should have been pretty pathetic, but somehow it wasn't. I looked at the pictures. Mr. and Mrs. John Hamlin on somebody's lawn. A little guy with a head too big for his stooped shoulders, his thin arm held in the possessive grip of a smirking, over-dressed Amazon.

Spike asked quietly: "Did Mr. Hamlin carry any insurance?"

"Yes. He took it out before we were married."

"A large amount?"

"Eighty thousand dollars."

Spike peered around the room.

"Quite a sizable policy for a man in his circumstances, wouldn't you say?"

I could see her stiffen as she glared at Spike. "Considering the dangers of his work, no. He wished me to be provided for if anything happened."

"Well, we'll hope his wish is granted," Spike said, rubbing a smile off his lips. "Although insurance companies sometimes get tough about things like this. Any further questions—children? If not, that will be all, Mrs. Hamlin. Sorry to trouble you, and thanks for the pictures."

We filed out, climbed into our cab and started back to the Hall.

"What a story, what a story!" Spike chortled. "If we can only crack it!"

"You mean this poor woman's losing her husband on their wedding anniversary?" Katie asked.

Spike moaned. "Brilliance. That's it. Positive brilliance. Duchess, don't you know a Schwartz when one jumps up and spits in your face?"

"A Schwartz?"

"Tell her, Pinky. She was still in kindergarten when the Schwartz case broke."

"This Schwartz was a chemist and inventor too," I said. "He had a laboratory out in Walnut Creek where he was working on a process of manufacturing artificial silk. One night there was an explosion and the joint burned down. They found a man's body in the ashes. Everybody thought, of course, that Schwartz had cashed his checks. His wife put in for the hundred grand insurance he carried.

"Then it developed that the body wasn't Schwartz's at all. The dead guy was an itinerant preacher whom the chemist had lured into the laboratory and knocked over the head. Schwartz, in the meantime, had holed up in an apartment he'd rented weeks before he pulled the hoax. The dicks got on his trail and were closing in on him when Schwartz put a .45 slug between his eyes. Since then, Katie, an insurance hoax of that type has been known as a Schwartz."

The Duchess took one of my cigarettes and lit it with hands that weren't very steady. "And you think this is an insurance hoax?"

"Cinch," Spike declared flatly.

"Why?"

"Because it's too damned pat and because that guy Hamlin carried too much insurance."

"And who was the man they found in the laboratory?"

"Some hobo who'll never be missed. Hamlin got him in there on the pretext of giving him a job, slapped him over the conk and fired the joint. Simple, Duchess."

"And you think Kurt Bergstrom was in on the hoax?" Katie pursued.

"Cinch." Spike nodded gleefully. "The way I dope it, the time of the fire was prearranged to put Bergstrom in the clear. John Hamlin is a weak sister and the whole plot was cooked up by Bergstrom and Mrs. Hamlin. Hamlin is safely holed up somewhere, and when the heat is off he and the dame'll scram to South America with forty grand."

"And the other forty grand?"

"Into Kurt Bergstrom's sock. Well, what do you think of it, Duchess?"

"I think the whole thing," Katie promptly retorted, "is a silly machination of a disordered brain."

WHEN WE GOT back to the press room I called the beat while Spike and the Duchess phoned their offices. Then, on a hunch, I rang the morgue and by sheer good luck got hold of the coroner himself.

"Pinky Kane," I said. "Look, coroner. About that man who was burned to death in the Bergstrom fire. Have you got around to a p.m. yet?"

"We've made a cursory examination at the request of Captain Wallis."

"What'd you find?"

"Perhaps you'd better ask Wallis. He ordered me not to give out any details."

Katie and Spike were still in the phone booths as I impatiently jiggled the hook, got the operator and asked for the Captain of Detectives. Wallis came on almost immediately.

"This is Kane, skipper. Understand you ordered a post mortem on Hamlin's body."

"That's right, Pinky."

"What'd you find out?"

"Well, his height and build approximate that of John Hamlin. He carried a gold watch on which Hamlin's initials are still discernible. He wore a full denture—not a tooth in his head. Same as Hamlin. And that, Kane, is about the works."

"Come on, skipper. Kick in."

"I said that was the works."

"Now look here. You were on that Schwartz case and so was I. And I haven't forgotten it. Now what else did your medical examiner discover when he went over that body? Tell me everything."

"Well," Captain Wallis sighed, "you'll get it sooner or later, so I might as well give it to you now. The man's skull had been fractured."

"Uh-huh, I thought you were holding out something like that. Hamlin's skull couldn't have been cracked in the fire, could it?"

"Chief Murphy said nothing fell on him and if he had a fractured skull he must have got it before the fire broke out."

"Well, what do you think?" I asked.

"I don't know how you spotted it, Pinky, but I think you're on the right track. Another Schwartz."

"How about Bergstrom? Do you think he's in on it?"

"If I answered that question I'd be guessing. So let's pass it."

"And Mrs. Hamlin?"

"I've only talked to her on the phone. She may be a party to the hoax and she may not. Probably not. Schwartz's wife wasn't, you know. He planned to contact her after the pay-off and, as the saying goes, tell all. Anyway, I've just sent out an all-state teletype with Hamlin's description. I've ordered him held."

"On what charge, skipper?"

"Murder, my boy. Murder," Captain Wallis said cheerfully.

I hung up, a bit breathless all of a sudden.

The Captain certainly had been working fast.

Katie came out of the *Sun* booth. "You've been talking to Bodie Wallis, haven't you?" she said, smiling.

"Bodie did most of the talking. I listened. He's sent out an all-state teletype to pick up John Hamlin."

Katie's laugh told me what she thought of Bodie Wallis. "John Hamlin has already been picked up. In a basket, by a couple of coroner's deputies."

"Captain Wallis doesn't think so."

"String with Captain Wallis, Pinky, and you'll sleep in the street," she said airily.

Spike tumbled out of the telephone booth bellowing:

"Hey, Pink! The office just got a flash from Duke Wayland on the lower beat. Captain Wallis—"

"I know. I was just talking to him."

"That guy had a fractured skull!" Spike exclaimed excitedly.

"Yeah," I said.

Katie's jaw dropped as she looked from Spike to me. "What guy had a fractured skull?" she asked in a small voice.

"The guy they picked up in a basket. The guy you were dumb enough to think was John Hamlin."

KATIE SAT DOWN abruptly. Spike and I stood looking at her, gloating a little. It wasn't often that the Duchess put her money on the wrong number.

"Well, muh frand?" Spike grinned at last.

She shrugged. "It looks bad but it isn't hopeless. I'm banking on one thing: the integrity of Kurt Bergstrom. I've known him for several years and I can't see him getting mixed up in an insurance hoax involving murder. And I can't see that meek and mild person, John Hamlin, hitting a man over the head and burning his body."

"That's logic for you," Spike jeered. "Kurt Bergstrom looks too honest to go in for murder. And John Hamlin looks too meek to kill anybody. Forget, for a minute, the looks of those two guys and where are you? Well, I'll tell you. You're stringing along with Pinky and me and Captain Wallis."

"Three," Katie said sarcastically, "of the most brilliant minds in the city. Well, if you three are brilliant, I'm a low moron. Good night."

Katie breezed, slamming the door.

Spike chuckled. "Did we get the little lady's goat, all right. But I'd much rather get John Hamlin."

"And maybe you think we won't. Now look. It's a ten to one shot the guy never left the city. His best bet was to establish a residence in some quiet apartment house. He's probably had the apartment for weeks, just like Schwartz did. All right. So what?"

"I'll bite."

"We smoke him out."

"You and me?"

"Don't be a sap. We got a staff, haven't we. We got three
or four cubs sitting over there in the office wearing out the
seats of their pants, haven't we? Oke! Tomorrow morning
early we turn 'em loose, along with anybody else Andy can
spare. We contact every hotel and apartment and rooming
house in the city."

"The dicks will be doing just that," I pointed out.

"What of it? We can put as many men on the job as
Bodie Wallis. We got just as good a chance as he has of
turning up Hamlin. And if we get a break—well, will
Katie's face be red? Dunt esk!"

WE WENT TO work the next morning. It was house-to-
house stuff and it was tiring. But we didn't care. Spike and
I felt, the whole *Telegram* staff felt, that we were on the
right track.

As we read John Hamlin's mind, he never expected any
hue and cry. He thought the corpse would be accepted as
his, and the pay-off would be a pushover. He'd made only
one mistake. He'd hit the poor devil he'd hired to double
for him too hard a blow. The body wasn't wholly consumed,
as he'd expected it to be, and the skull fracture showed up
in the post mortem. John Hamlin, we reasoned, must have
got quite a shock when he read the papers in the morning
and learned that every law enforcement officer in the state
was looking for him.

It was a long hard day and we found no trace of John
Hamlin. Something, however, was in our blood. The thrill
of the chase. We felt, Spike and I and the cubs, as though
surely we'd locate him in the next apartment house, the

next hotel. We kept doggedly at it all day, all the day following, all the day after that.

At five in the afternoon of the third day, dead on my feet, I strolled into the City Hall press room. The reporters on the afternoon papers had gone home and Katie, looking fresh and spruce and more than a little like a million dollars, was all alone.

"You looked dragged out, Pinky," she smiled. "Where have you been all day?"

"Hunting John Hamlin," I said, slumping into a chair.

"Why, don't you read the papers? Hamlin was buried today. I covered the funeral."

I sighed. "You don't really think that was Hamlin, do you? I know you're silly, Duchess, and I know your judgment isn't very good. But you're not that silly, are you?"

She looked at me hard for a long minute. Then:

"See here, Pinky Kane. I don't like that. I don't like it even a little bit. You can call me almost anything else, but I draw the line at being called silly. I was going to spare you this, but on second thought I won't. I'll go out of my way, for once, just to show you how silly *you* are. Will you meet me at the Drake Hotel at eight tonight?"

"What for?"

"For the pay-off," Katie said.

The door had opened and Spike Kaylor stood on the threshold. "Where's the pay-off?" he demanded.

"At the Drake, tonight," the Duchess told him. "You're invited.

"Thanks," Spike grinned. "Will this affair be formal, or shall I—"

"Wear tails, by all means," Katie shot back, and left the room.

"What's the kid got on her mind?" Spike asked.

"You can't prove anything by me."

"Do you really think she has a hot lead?"

"I wouldn't put it beyond her."

"But what is it? She hasn't found John Hamlin, has she?"

"No. She insists Hamlin is dead and buried."

"But maybe that's just to throw us off the track." Spike eased into a chair. "Pay-off, huh? Pay-off," he mused. "Pink, there's something screwy about this picture. If she was ready to crack this story, would she invite us to the party? Not any! She'd tell us something was due to pop and let us stew in our own juices until two o'clock tomorrow morning when the final edition of the *Sun* comes out."

"That's what you'd think, all right. So what?"

"So we take her up. What the hell else can we do?"

We found the Duchess, sitting off by herself, in the lobby of the Drake at eight o'clock.

"Well, keed, when does the curtain go up?" Spike asked.

"Almost any minute," Katie returned shortly. "Just keep your shirts on and your mouths shut."

She lit a fresh cigarette off a glowing butt.

Her hands were shaking and I saw that the palms were moist. Her eyes were bright, feverish, as she kept watching the door.

"Our little pal seems a bit nervous," Spike grinned.

"We can do without your puerile mouthings for a while, Mr. Kaylor," the Duchess told him.

THEN KURT BERGSTROM strode into the lobby and Katie rose. The chemist spotted her and came over. He looked keyed up and he didn't smile as he bowed perfunctorily over her hand.

"These are your friends?" he asked, looking at Spike and me with cold and fishy eyes.

"Not my friends, but they'll do as witnesses."

"Goot! Bring them up in ten minutes." Bergstrom turned and walked briskly toward the elevators. Katie sat down and lit another cigarette. She was plenty nervous.

I began to feel restive myself. Even Spike, who is almost irrepressible, didn't have anything to say. We watched ten slow minutes tick off on the clock over the desk. Then Katie stood up.

"When we go up to Bergstrom's room," she said, "you two will do as you're told and ask no questions. Have you got that straight?"

"Oke, kid," Spike nodded. "Lead the way." Bergstrom received us in the living room of his suite. He waved Katie to a chair and then stood for a minute eyeing Spike and me. You could see he didn't like us. You could see he wished we were a long way from there. Finally he said:

"I hope we can trust them, Miss Blayne."

"They'll do as they're told and like it," the Duchess said.

"That all depends," Spike said, "on what you tell us to do."

Bergstrom threw open a door to a clothes closet. "You will go in there und stay there und keep quiet," he said crisply. "You will leaf the door oben two or three inches, joost enough so you can see und hear what goes on. You will nod come oudt until you are told to come oudt. All right?"

"All right," Spike agreed.

"I will tell you when to go in. In the meantime, please to sit down und be comfortable."

We sat down diffidently. So help me, I couldn't get the angle. I couldn't make head or tail of the layout. Spike caught my eye, while Bergstrom paced briskly up and down the room, and signalled: "Watch yourself. I don't trust this guy." I didn't trust him either.

After a time the telephone rang. Bergstrom took it up, listened a moment, ordered: "Show him up at once."

Spike started to rise.

"No, no. Nod yet," Bergstrom said irritably. "It iss only Captain Wallis."

Spike sat down again, looking a bit deflated. Bodie Wallis came in after a few minutes. In his quiet blue serge business suit, he didn't look much like a detective.

He nodded to Katie and Bergstrom, grinned at Spike and me.

"You two boys don't miss anything, do you?" he chuckled.

"Not if we can help it," Spike admitted, a bit boastfully.

"I might point out," Katie remarked, "that they are here at my invitation. And anything they see or hear won't be reported in the *Telegram* until it has appeared exclusively in the *Sun*. Right, Mr. Kaylor?"

"Wrong, Miss Blayne!" Spike bristled. "That wasn't part of the bargain."

"It's part of the bargain now."

"Sister, it takes two to make a bargain. And as long as I have two legs and can run to the nearest telephone—"

THE PHONE BUZZED at that instant and Bergstrom raised his hand authoritatively. "Silence, if you please!" He picked up the instrument, and after a moment: "Show her up at once."

He turned and waved us toward the closet. We got up and went in and closed the door to a two-inch crack. Spike jammed his foot against the door and I pulled on the knob, to hold it steady open. Spike, kneeling at the crack, whispered:

"It's a funny one, Pink. You got any ideas?"

"No ideas, but I got a good hunch," I whispered. "Bergstrom is on the spot. With Katie's unwitting help, he's trying to slide out from under."

"Yeah. That's the way I dope it. He's about to pull a fast one. And when it comes down the groove, we'll pole it over the right-field fence for a home run. How's about it?"

"That's okay by me."

We didn't say any more, because Bergstrom had stepped to the hall door and was admitting—Mrs. John Hamlin! She wore black and she looked tense and watchful and cool. Bergstrom was saying:

"Miss Blayne you haff met, I believe. Und this, Mrs. Hamlin, iss Mr. Wallis."

Mister Wallis! Well, why not? The whole situation was cockeyed anyway.

"Please to sit down, Mrs. Hamlin," Bergstrom said, helping her to a chair with great solicitude. "We haff wonderful news for you. Your husband, my dear, iss *alive!*"

Mrs. Hamlin sat on the edge of her chair, stiffly, blinking up at him. She said carefully: "I buried my husband this afternoon."

Bergstrom smiled down at her gently, shook his head. "The man you buried vas nod your husband. John iss alive.

He vas badly burned in the fire und he sustained a severe injury to the head. He hass been suffering from amnesia ever since. In fact, even now he iss delirious. But the doctor assures me that his chances for pulling through are excellent."

The woman never moved but I could see the last of the color in her cheeks fade out.

Spike whispered: "Amnesia! Did I tell you a fast one was coming down the groove? Amnesia!"

Well, it was easy enough for a couple of smart reporters to dope the play. I saw it this way: When Bergstrom and Hamlin realized their hoax wasn't going over, they got together and devised this amnesia gag. Burned Hamlin with a little acid, probably. Cooked up a good story. "I don't remember anything that happened till I woke up in the hospital." That sort of thing—it's pulled every day.

YES, IT WAS all pretty smart. Just about the type of stuff you'd expect a bright lad like Herr Bergstrom to pull. Having Captain Wallis there on the job was just the right touch. It showed the supreme confidence and egoism of the chemist.

"I feel certain there has been some mistake," Mrs. Hamlin said slowly, gripping the arms of her chair. "I did not see John's body. I did not want to look at it. But I knew, as I sat there staring at the coffin this afternoon, that my husband was in it."

"But," Bergstrom pointed out calmly, "there iss no way you *could* know, Mrs. Hamlin. No way in the world, because—John iss in bed in the next room. Alive. Delirious, seriously burned, very ill—but *alive!*"

He shouted that last word in a way that sent a chill

down my spine—even though I'd suspected all along that Hamlin wasn't dead.

And then all at once I was conscious of a voice from the room on the far side. Someone in there had been talking for quite a while, talking very softly. And now, as Spike and I and the people in the living room listened, the voice grew louder. We could catch a word or two: "Valence of three ... calcium chloride ... neutralized ..."

What a shock to that woman who was sitting there so white and rigid. A voice, literally, from the dead!

I felt my hair standing on end. I heard Spike's fast and unsteady breathing. I could feel his body shaking with the tension of nerves about to snap. Let me tell you, it was electric!

Bergstrom stepped to the other door. He threw it open. The room was dark but we heard that rasping voice going on monotonously: "... carbon union in the aliphatic hydrocarbons has apparently the same effect on the boiling point as two hydrogen atoms. But as I was telling you, Kurt, an acetylenic or triple linkage is associated with a rise in the boiling point. However ..."

Mrs. Hamlin was on her feet, staring into the darkened room. She screamed: "No! No!"

Bergstrom said patiently, gently: "But yes, Mrs. Hamlin. Surely you recognize John's voice."

The woman caught the arm of a chair, steadied herself. "I tell you," she cried hysterically, "John is *dead!*"

"No. John iss very much alive."

Bergstrom reached inside the door, flipped the switch. The bedroom was bright with light. Looking straight across the living room, I could see a figure in the bed. I caught a glimpse of a head swathed in bandages. I saw lips moving. I heard the deadly monotonous voice going on and on.

"... true of the fatty acid series, Kurt, and the corresponding ketones and..."

THEN THE BEDROOM door was blocked by the angular figure of Mrs. Hamlin. She swayed against the frame, caught herself, screamed: "No, no, I tell you! It can't be true! He can't be alive! I killed him myself with a hammer. I got into the plant with a key to the back door. I've had it for months: I crept up behind him. I knocked him down. I poured gasoline over him and struck a match. I saw him burn. *I saw him burn!*"

All this in a wild screech that sent icy chills up and down my spine. John Hamlin's voice went on:

"... although, Kurt, the correlation of melting point with constitution has not..."

The tall woman covered her face with her angular hands. She screamed through her bony fingers: *"I tell you I killed him!"*

Then she dropped in a dead faint.

"... symmetry of the resulting molecule may exert such a lowering effect that the final result..."

"Westoby!" Bergstrom yelled, "Ged out uf bed und turn that damn' thing off. If I haff to listen to John Hamlin's voice one minute longer I shall haff hysterics!"

Well, after Mrs. Hamlin had snapped out of her faint and Captain Wallis had taken her away, we were all pretty limp. Bergstrom brought out a bottle and some ice, and we all sat down and tried to come back to Earth. The chemist remarked finally:

"Fortunately, Hamlin had been helping me with my

sount devize. I suppose I haff a mile or two uf film on which his voice iss recorded."

Westoby, who is one of the chemist's lab men, added: "Lucky, too, the film was stored in the physical laboratory in the south wing, which the fire didn't touch."

The Duchess was smiling. "And speaking of luck, wasn't it a break that I brushed against Mrs. Hamlin's coat in her hallway the other night?"

"Huh?" Spike grunted. "What's Mrs. Hamlin's coat got to do with it?"

"It was wet, darling," Katie said pleasantly. "There were beads of rain on the fur collar. And Mrs. Hamlin had told us she hadn't left the house that evening."

"Look here!" Spike snorted. "Do you mean to tell me you had the play doped from the beginning?"

"I had it doped, as you put it, within an hour or two after I brushed against that wet coat."

"Well, Duchess, I got to hand it to you. You're the top." He drained his glass and stood up. "Bergstrom, you've put on a grand show and we'll give your sound recorder a million dollars' worth of publicity. Now I've got to hit a phone with the story. Okay to use yours?"

"No," Bergstrom said steadily. "It iss most decidedly nod okay to use mine."

"Huh?" Spike gasped. "Wha-zat?"

Bergstrom, still smiling, bowed to Katie. And the Duchess rose.

"Mr. Bergstrom has ordered the operator to accept no out-going calls," she informed us. "So if you want to give your office the story, Spike, you'll have to find another telephone."

She moved toward the door, adding over her shoulder: "If you can, and that will be quite a job!"

"If I can!" Spike bellowed, and started after her. "While I've got the use of my legs, I guess—"

Katie threw open the door. Lounging in the hall outside I caught a glimpse of half a dozen of the toughest looking punks I ever saw outside of a penitentiary—or a morning paper's circulation department. Spike stopped in his tracks.

"Keep them here, boys, until midnight," the Duchess ordered cheerfully. "And try not to hurt them too badly if they make a break."

"We won't hurt 'em, Miss Katie," a big bruiser grinned. "Not *much!*"

Well, they didn't hurt us—because we didn't make a break. We stayed there till midnight, drinking very good whiskey with Kurt Bergstrom and wondering where we ever got the idea that the Duchess was silly, and dumb, and slow on the pick-up.

MURDER AT REHEARSAL

*Katie Blayne, the Duchess, Set Too Fast
a Pace to Please the City Hall News-
Hounds—but After That Murder Frame,
They Would Go the Limit for Her Any Time*

1

A FUNNY THING—THE three of us were sitting in the City
Hall press room discussing them at the exact moment, as
we learned later, the murder was committed.

We were talking about Abner Holt, wealthy amateur
actor and patron of the arts. We were talking about Harriet
Holt, Abner's youthful wife, who was the leading lady
of the Community Players. We were talking, too, about
young Sam O'Malley, director of the Community Theater.
O'Malley had been imported by Abner Holt, at ten grand
a year, to make us yokels Drahma-conscious.

And we were talking, as usual, about Katie Blayne,
known to a dubious fame as the Duchess. Katie covers
police for the *Sun*.

We were talking about these four, collectively so to
speak, because Katie had the second lead in the Players'
forthcoming production and was spending this afternoon,
her day off, at rehearsal.

Sour-faced Jeff Gervin, of the *Sentinel*, shuffled the
cards viciously. "Look here, you lugs. I say there's something phony about the Duchess giving this acting racket a
tumble. I'll lay even money she's got a crush on Handsome
Sam—O'Malley to you."

Spike Kaylor snapped: "Deal, will yuh?"

Jeff dealt, picked up his hand, sorted it, and cocked a

mean eye at me. "Katie," he said, "always was a sucker for the collar-ad type. Too bad, Pinky, you got such big ears and that busted nose."

"Would you just as soon lay off the Duchess for a while?" Spike demanded. He's a little guy and when he gets peevish his short-cropped bushy red hair seems to stand up all over his head. "I'm sick of hearing about the dame. Bid!"

The game finally got under way. And fifteen minutes later, in the middle of a hot hand, the desk sergeant poked his head in the press room doorway.

"Look, fellows! I guess you'll want this. I just got a flash from the inspectors' bureau. Katie Blayne has killed Abner Holt. Shot him in the heart at the Community Theater. Captain Wallis has just gone out. I thought you'd like to know."

And he ducked through the door...

No one of us said anything. I found myself staring blankly at Jeff Gervin, without seeing him. And then his hard face with the thin lips, the little black eyes, the bushy eyebrows one higher than the other, swam into focus.

He was looking at me with one cocked eye. He was leering at me! His lips twisted downward. He said: "So that's the dame you got a crush on. A killer, huh? Nice girl!"

I realized all at once that my right fist was moving. I put my shoulder behind it and landed flush on his sneering mouth. Jeff toppled backwards in his chair and struck the floor with a crash.

Faster than I'd ever moved before in my life I got out of there.

I found Captain Wallis' big black sedan drawn up in front of the Community Theater. Pulling in behind it, I

"My father—and a devil. He's ruined my life and yours"

cut my motor, leaped out, dashed up the stairs and into the theater.

The house was dark but the stage was bright with light and crowded with people. I started down the aisle on a dead run. Then I slowed to a walk and at last I was barely moving.

For abruptly it seemed to me that the darkened house was full of tense and silent people who were watching the steady unfolding of a vital drama. Like a late arrival, mindful of the rights of the rest of the audience, I crept to a seat in the front row and eased silently into it.

Get the setting, the characters:

A drawing room. A chesterfield set diagonally center. A table beside it. An occasional chair to right, another to left, two at the rear. Several bridge lamps. Fireplace right. Door downstage from it. Another door, open, at left.

Downstage right, the body of Abner Holt. Beside it,

kneeling, Captain Wallis. On the other side of the body, standing, looking dumb and important, Inspector Jenkins.

On the chesterfield, Harriet Holt, sobbing but not hysterical. On either side of her a young man and a young woman I'd never seen before. Behind the chesterfield, slouching, a gangly man in overalls.

At the rear, pacing nervously back and forth, handsome, dark-eyed Sam O'Malley. To the left upstage, a group of three young people I didn't know.

And motionless beside the davenport table, white but not excited, watching Captain Wallis with steady eyes, Katie Blayne, blond and slim and lovely.

THERE WAS NO sound, for the moment, except the quiet sobbing of the dead man's wife. Captain Wallis rose slowly to his feet; he was old and you could almost hear his bones creak. He turned to the Duchess, gave her a long stare from those ice-blue eyes of his and tossed her the cue:

"Start from the beginning, Katie. And make it snappy."

Katie took a step forward toward the footlights. She was beautiful and tragic; she had poise. Her acting was—

But this wasn't acting! This was living. Abner Holt wasn't lying motionless, trying not to show he breathed. Abner Holt was dead! The red stuff on the stage beside his still body was blood!

Katie, steadily: "It was our final rehearsal before our performance tonight. I won't bother you with the details of the play. Suffice to say that Mrs. Holt and I were alone on the stage. The others were not off-stage, but merely in the background, out of the way. The action called for Mr. Holt to come out of that door right. I am across the stage.

There are two or three brief lines. Then I take a gun out of my handbag and shoot him. Well—"

Katie faltered; she got hold of herself, continued evenly. "He came out, we read our lines, I fired at him and—he fell. He screamed once and—and died!"

Captain Wallis, with heavy sarcasm: "I see. And the revolver, of course, was supposed to have been loaded with a blank cartridge."

Katie, defiantly: "The revolver was loaded with a blank cartridge. I loaded it myself just before we started to run through the scene. And please don't suggest, Captain, that I don't know a blank cartridge from the other kind."

Captain Wallis, sneering: "Yeah. Sure, sure. But there's Abner Holt. Dead. How would you account for it?"

Katie, helplessly: "I don't, Captain."

Inspector Jenkins, edging downstage: "It's a cinch, skipper. After the Duchess loaded the rod with the blank shell, somebody slipped out the phony and put in the real McCoy."

Katie, smiling faintly: "It's a good theory, Inspector. But I loaded the revolver only a minute or two before I fired the shot. And from the time I loaded it and put it in my handbag until the time I took it out and fired, the gun wasn't out of my possession for an instant."

I heard the patter of footsteps. Turning, I saw Spike Kaylor and Jeff Gervin rearing down out of the gloom of the darkened house. I hissed at them:

"S-s-s-s! Sit down, you mugs. Sit down and keep quiet."

They eased into seats across the aisle, silently almost apologetically. I don't think any of the people on the stage had heard my admonition, or even knew they had an audience.

The play went on as Captain Wallis said coldly:

"If you say, Miss Blayne, that the gun was never out of your possession from the time you loaded it with the blank until you fired it, there is only one other explanation of this killing." He paused an instant, trying to stare her down with those cold blue eyes of his. I could have killed him! "Someone off stage shot Holt at the exact instant you fired the blank."

O'Malley, speaking for the first time: "Such timing, Captain, would be impossible. I am a director. I understand timing. I know that for those two shots to have coincided they must have been fired within a tenth of a second of each other. Perhaps less. No one, standing off stage, could time a shot to coincide so closely with the instant Miss Blayne pulled the trigger. It is impossible."

Captain Wallis, coldly: "Then there is only one alternative."

I held my breath, and everybody else in the theater seemed to do the same thing, as Wallis went on:

"You, Miss Blayne, gave a signal to the party off stage. A certain movement of the gun, say. Or a slight movement of your left hand, or your head. You—and the party off stage—had rehearsed this signal until your timing was perfect. And the two explosions were so nearly simultaneous that the other people on the stage thought they heard only one shot."

There was a taut and breathless silence. I saw Katie's lips go white and her blue eyes, for an instant, were frightened.

Then her head lifted a little and her jaw hardened with determination.

Katie, steadily and coldly: "You are accusing me, then, of complicity in a cold-blooded murder?"

O'Malley, angrily: "You're being absurd, Captain!"

Inspector Jenkins: "Shut up, you! The Captain's conductin' this investigation."

O'Malley: "But, you addle-pated idiots—"

Katie: "Please, Mr. O'Malley! You won't do me any good by calling them names."

2

HARRIET HOLT, SPEAKING for the first time: "I think you're all crazy. Miss Blayne and my husband were the best of friends. Why, what possible motive—"

Inspector Jenkins, threateningly: "Skip it!"

Captain Wallis, decisively: "It is too soon, Mrs. Holt, to delve into motives. All we want now is to construct a reasonable theory to explain the commission of this murder." Wallis nodded toward the revolver which lay on the table: "Who, by the way, belongs to the gun?"

O'Malley: "It belongs to me. I like guns and I have several good ones."

Inspector Jenkins: "You got permits for these several good guns you got?"

O'Malley: "I have permits to own and to carry every one of them."

Captain Wallis, glaring first at the body and then at Katie: "Well, that's the way it stands. Either Miss Blayne signaled someone off stage to fire at the instant she pulled the trigger, or the cartridge she herself put in the gun was not a blank."

O'Malley, fiercely: "And either way you're accusing the girl of murder!"

Captain Wallis, bellowing angrily: "I'm accusing no one of anything—yet! So just keep your mouth shut." More quietly: "One point will be settled within a day, however. Miss Blayne may or may not have lied about the cartridge she put in the gun. But the marks made by the lands of the rifling will not lie. As soon as the lethal bullet is recovered, I'll put our ballistics expert to work. By tomorrow, at the latest, we'll know whether or not the shot came from that revolver on the table. That will be all."

I heard Jeff Gervin mutter: "Curtain!"

The first act was over.

Five minutes later I was driving down the street with Katie Blayne beside me. She didn't look much like a fine actress now. She looked like a scared little girl who wanted to cry. I put my arm around her and pulled her over against me.

"Try to forget about it, kid. You haven't killed anybody and we all know it."

She didn't say anything; she merely sighed. And it struck me all at once that the Duchess didn't know, didn't truly know, whether she had killed Abner Holt or not. What a spot for a nice kid like Katie!

"Look, Duchess! Are you absolutely certain you put a blank in that gun?"

She drew away from me. "Pinky? Don't be a fool! Is that the sort of thing a person would make a mistake about?"

"All right, we'll pass that. And you are sure, too, that the gun wasn't out of your possession from the time you loaded it until you fired it."

"You heard me tell Captain Wallis, didn't you, that I was absolutely certain?"

"Telling Captain Wallis is one thing. Telling me is

another. And being absolutely certain is still a third. Now, what'll you have? I'll take vanilla."

"This is no time, Pinky, for smart cracks. I tell you the gun was never out of my possession for an instant."

"Then somebody in the wings contrived to fire at the same instant you did."

"And the timing?"

"Who knows? Blind luck, maybe."

"No," Katie said. "People who set out to commit cold-blooded murders don't trust to blind luck."

"All right. Who had a motive to kill Abner Holt? His wife?"

"So far as I know, Harriet loved him. She's quite a bit younger than he, but she's always been comradely and loyal."

"All right, who else? Sam O'Malley?"

"Mr. Holt brought Sam O'Malley out here from Detroit at a high salary. As long as Holt lived, Sam O'Malley would have a good position. Now that he's dead, O'Malley will probably have to look for a job. Is it likely that Sam would kill that kind of a patron?"

"It doesn't seem so. Who else? Who was the guy in overalls?"

"Grogan, I think his name is. He's just a stage electrician on hand for the dress rehearsal. I see no reason why he'd kill Mr. Holt."

"No, none of us see any reason why anybody would kill Mr. Holt," I said bitterly. "But somebody did. It wasn't an accident. You're too positive about that revolver and you know too much about firearms. So what?"

"So, darling, suppose you drop me at the *Sun* office." She

tried to speak lightly, but she didn't have much spirit. "After all, you know, my dream, the dream of every good reporter, has come true. I was on the scene when a big story broke." She choked on the words. "And I've got—to write—an eye-witness story."

I DROPPED HER at the *Sun* building and then phoned my office. When I got back to the press room in the City Hall, Jeff Gervin and Spike were there, along with half a dozen other reporters and a couple of photographers.

"You're a pal," Jeff beefed, "stealing the star suspect before we could get a camera man on the job. Do you realize there isn't a paper in town, outside of the *Sun*, that has Katie's picture in its morgue?"

"And there isn't a paper in town, outside of your lousy sheet, that would use Katie's picture," Spike spoke up, bristling.

Jeff shrugged, turned to his desk and dragged out a bottle. He took a husky snort and cocked one eye at me.

"I'll see you in court, big boy," he leered, heading toward the door, "when the Duchess goes on trial for murder."

Well, that was a laugh—but not a very big one.

The next day Katie was on the job as usual. She looked dragged out, as though she hadn't slept much, and she started nervously whenever a door banged or a phone rang. No one mentioned the case, but we were all of us pretty jittery.

We kept wondering what would be the conclusion of Captain Wallis' ballistic expert. If Katie had actually fired the shot that killed Abner Holt—

Well, that was something I didn't like to think about. Frankly, I was scared.

It was a little after eleven when I answered one of the phones and recognized Captain Wallis' cold voice. "Is Miss Blayne there?"

"Yes."

"All right, keep her there. I'll be down."

I hung up and looked at Katie. Her eyes, meeting mine, were haggard, frightened. Her mouth trembled. Damn it, I felt as though someone were twisting a knife in my heart!

"It was Bodie Wallis," I said. "Now look here, Duchess. Keep a stiff upper lip. No matter what happens, we're for you. We may have been pretty nasty to you sometimes, and resented you, and all that. But when the pinch comes, we're backing you up. Right, gang?"

"Right," Spike Kaylor loyally agreed.

"Absolutely," nodded lanky, hatchet-faced Pete Zerker of the *Bulletin*.

"O.K.," said fat Willie Blake of the *Sentinel*.

"Oh, nuts," Jeff Gervin snorted.

The Duchess gripped the arms of her chair, said quietly to the room at large:

"Listen. This is going against me. I have a feeling. Captain Wallis is going to tell me the bullet came from my gun. Now listen. I thought of something, lying awake last night. I thought of two things. First, the recoil of that shot was very slight. Now you know there is almost no kick from a blank cartridge. It's a matter of weight. To every action there is an equal and opposite reaction."

"Hurry up, kid," I urged.

"Well, with no bullet, only a paper wadding, there is very little recoil. That's the first thing that proves the bullet didn't come out of that gun. Here's the second. I'm almost certain I wasn't aiming at Mr. Holt when I pulled the trigger. He was more than halfway across the stage from me. But even so, I thought of the paper wadding. I thought of Mr. Holt's eyes. And I know I aimed to the right of him."

"That," Willie Blake said, "should cinch the matter."

"In my own mind, yes. But those are hard things to prove. Now look. Shall I tell Captain Wallis all this if he says I fired the bullet?"

"Kid, if he says that, you're going to need an attorney," I said.

"Tell Wallis nothing," Spike growled.

"Tell your attorney," Pete ordered.

Jeff Gervin poured himself a drink and didn't make any comments. I strolled over to him.

"Look, Jeff."

"At what?"

"You're not sounding off. Not any. You're not spilling what Katie has told us either to your lousy paper or to Brodie Wallis. Got it?"

He looked at me with narrowed eyes, sneering. "Yeah."

"Then keep it."

"And if you don't," Spike Kaylor vowed, "there'll be another murder mystery around here"

Captain Wallis came in carrying a sheaf of photographs, still wet. He nodded to us, scowling, and laid out the pictures on Willie's desk.

"You boys all know the procedure," he said. "Twelve photographs of the lethal bullet, spaced thirty degrees apart, and joined together to make a long strip. A similar composite photograph of a slug from the suspected weapon. Place one strip above the other, move it back and forth, try to match up the grooves made by the lands of the rifling. Now the rifling of no two guns is identical. Just as—"

"Sure," Spike Kaylor interrupted impatiently, "just as no two fingerprints are identical. Greatly enlarged, gentlemen of the jury, as are these photographs I now hold in my hand— Aw, nuts! We know all that stuff, Bodie. What's the verdict? Did the bullet that killed Abner Holt come out of the gun Katie fired?"

We held our breaths as Captain Wallis jerked his head toward the array of pictures.

"It did," he said coldly. "You may look for yourselves."

I reached for Katie too late. Out cold, she slid down in a little heap on the littered floor of the press room.

Willie came over, as I put her head down and Pete ran for water. "Jeez, the poor kid," Willie said. "Even if she didn't mean to kill him, even if somebody jobbed her, it's a hell of a thing to have on her conscience. Jeez!"

3

WHEN WE HAD finally brought Katie around and got her into a chair and a little color had come back in her face, Captain Wallis strolled over. He stood looking at her with those sharp cold blue eyes that had made many a crook's heart quail.

"Got anything more to say, Katie?"

"Nothing. Only what I told you yesterday."

"That's your story and you're sticking to it, huh? How about these pictures?"

Katie shrugged helplessly and bit her lip. I knew that if she said anything she'd burst into tears.

Wallis stood glaring at her. I could have swung on him! He said finally: "I'm not making any pinch right now, Katie. However, if the conclusion pointed by those pictures, along with what we've said here, gets into any of the papers—into the can you go."

He looked at us and we looked at Jeff Gervin.

Jeff poured himself a drink and hissed:

"Sissies!"

"Now, here's my plan," Wallis went on. "I want to spend the rest of the day checking up on the people who were in the theater when Holt was shot. Grogan, the electrician, for instance. The others members of the cast. Then tonight we'll have a rehearsal in the Community Theater.

You newspapermen and myself will make up the audience. The cast will be as you saw it yesterday.

"Miss Blayne and the other players will take their places on the stage, just where they were when that last scene was begun. You'll start, Katie, from the point you make your entrance for that scene. You'll carry through to the point where you fired at Holt. And we'll see what happens. We'll see who lied about where he was at that moment. We'll check every member of the cast against every other member. Somebody lied, and when we find a liar in a situation like this—well, we find a murderer. That's all."

The captain went out. And after a little while Jeff Gervin started to follow him. Spike Kaylor stopped him at the door.

"Where you bound, mugg?"

"That," said Jeff, "is my business. If I'm wrong, correct me."

"Then consider yourself corrected. Where you bound?"

Jeff was half drunk and he had, certainly, provocation. He swung a long looping right that clipped Spike behind the ear and sent him spinning. The rest of us were sitting down. Before we could get to our feet and bar the door, Jeff Gervin was out and gone.

"Now isn't that a pretty kettle of fish?" Willie Blake groaned.

Spike picked himself up, nodded to me and we went out into the corridor.

"Look here, Pink," Spike began. "That little gal is in a tough spot. We gotta help her."

Coming from Spike Kaylor, this was something. Spike has never liked the Duchess.

"Why should you worry?" I asked. "After the way you've treated the kid since she's been in the press room."

"Have I been lousy?" Spike grinned. "Well, that was all in the spirit of real clean fun. Well, fairly clean, anyway. This is different. Jeff Gervin, if I know that rat, has gone to work to hang this job on the Duchess. And while Jeff may be a drunk and all that, he's a damned sharp newspaperman and a top-notch investigator. If anybody can hang it on her, Jeff can do it."

"Not to mention that damned Captain Wallis. He'd hang a murder on his own mother to make page one."

"You said it."

"All right. What's to do?" I asked.

"I want you to cover the beat for me today. I gotta hunch."

"Shoot!"

"Shoot hell! There's been too much shooting on this job already. Do you cover for me today?"

"I cover for you today."

When I went back into the press room Katie was sitting in a chair, just sitting there staring at the opposite wall and looking white and frightened, sick. It must be a jolt to be told all of a sudden that you have, all unwittingly, killed a decent and honorable man.

I wanted to say something to cheer her, but, so help me, I couldn't think of a thing. I was sunk.

Spike Kaylor, a cub reporter, had a hunch. That was one side of the case. And on the other side—Jeff Gervin, mean, vindictive, but a brilliant mind and a crack reporter, also had a hunch. And Captain Wallis, nobody's fool, was out to make a record for himself.

That was the situation. Was it any wonder I couldn't think of anything cheering to say?

AT EIGHT O'CLOCK that evening I sat with Willie Blake, Jeff Gervin, Peter Zerker and three or four other newspapermen, in the front row of the Community Theater.

"Where's Spike?" Willie asked.

"Haven't seen him since morning," I said. "He had a hunch and went to work on it."

Jeff Gervin guffawed. "That cub? Listen. I saw Spike Kaylor in Mike's jernt half an hour ago. And was he cockeyed? Been drinking all day, if you ask me."

That hit me hard. Well, if Jeff Gervin told the truth, I'd knock Spike Kaylor's head off the next time I saw him.

"And lemme tell you something else, you chicken-hearted lugs," Jeff Gervin went on. "When this case is cracked, I'll crack it. Me and Bodie Wallis. And when we crack it, muh franz, the Duchess goes to jail!"

"And when'll that be, mugg?" I asked.

"Pretty damned quick!"

He said it with such evident glee, such smug confidence, that all at once I felt a sinking in the pit of my stomach. My hands were wet with perspiration, and yet I shivered.

Was Jeff Gervin bluffing? Taking us for a ride? Or was he in the know?

I looked up at Katie on the stage. I wanted to yell: "Don't go through with this farce! They're going to trick you! Don't say a word! Don't do a thing! Stop! Stop before it's too late!"

That's what I wanted to yell at Katie—and I did not have the nerve.

The house lights went off; the footlights went on. The show began.

Captain Wallis, from the orchestra pit: "You've all been told what you're supposed to do. O'Malley, you'll have to slip out of your own part and play Mr. Holt's. You probably know the lines better than anybody else. Do that at the point Mr. Holt comes on stage. All right. Go ahead."

The younger players and the overalled electrician walked to the rear of the stage. O'Malley moved up to the footlights, well to the right, and stood watching the action. Katie moved left to the door, leaving Harriet Holt alone on the chesterfield.

Katie: "Hello, Jane."

Harriet, rising in surprise: "Why, darling! Where in the world did you drop from?"

Katie, dully clutching her bag: "I didn't drop. I came up. From hell."

Harriet: "Oh, but darling! You shouldn't talk that way. Come over here and sit down. There must be a way out of this."

Katie: "There is a way. One way."

Harriet: "What do you mean?"

O'Malley, aside to Captain Wallis: "I'm going into Holt's part now." He slipped into the ring wing and came out the door onto the living room set. He was fumbling with a pair of glasses. "Ah. Ah. There you are, my dear. Damme, Jane, if I haven't broken my glasses again."

Harriet: "Dad! Here is Helen. Can't you speak to her?"

As O'Malley peered, blinking, across the stage at Katie I felt my heart pounding. The lid was about to blow off. I could feel it in every nerve of my body.

O'Malley, still peering across the stage: "Surely not—not *Helen!*"

Katie, bitterly: "Yes. Your darling Helen."

O'Malley took two faltering steps toward her. And Katie, on the other side of the stage, calmly opened her handbag. She took out the revolver without a word.

Harriet, screaming: "Helen! Helen! Don't. He's your own father!"

Katie: "Yes, and a devil. He's ruined my life and yours."

She raised the gun and fired at O'Malley.

And that, it seemed, was that. I felt let down, disappointed, like you feel when you go to a show expecting a hit and see a flop. There was no sense to it, no climax, no more drama than you'd find in an aquarium.

Captain Wallis said calmly: "Very well done, everybody. Now, Miss Blayne, if you will—"

4

AND SUDDENLY WE saw, we all saw, that Sam O'Malley was sinking to his knees, his hands clutching his right side, his face contorted.

I found myself on my feet. We were all on our feet.

Captain Wallis leaped onto a chair and started to climb over the footlights, muttering: "Good Lord! Good Lord!"

Katie Blayne's jaw had dropped and she stood staring blankly first at O'Malley and then at the revolver in her hand.

Harriet Holt, widow of a day, screamed and started for O'Malley. "Oh, my darling! My darling! What happened?"

O'Malley was on his knees. His face was dead white, his eyes terror-stricken.

Harriet Holt, this young and lovely widow, dropped to her knees beside him, pleading: "Tell me, darling! Are you badly hurt?"

Captain Wallis gained the stage; he was still muttering: "Good Lord! Good Lord!"

O'Malley raised his tragic Irish eyes. I guess he thought he was dying and he had to die prettily. "Harriet, dear! I'm shot!"

And then above the confused babble came a sneering, jeering voice from the wings:

"So it stung a little, did it? Hurt you, huh? Well, how do you think it felt to Abner Holt?"

And in the sudden dead and awesome silence, Spike Kaylor swaggered onto the stage. He carried a Lüger automatic fitted with a detachable butt and a Maxim silencer. His hat was on cock-eyed. A smoldering cigarette drooped from his lips. He looked pretty drunk, but he walked with an air.

Captain Wallis bellowed abruptly: "Kaylor! Have you shot this man?"

"Sure, Skipper, sure! But there wasn't enough powder behind that pellet to knock over a hummingbird. Prob'ly didn't even break the skin. It just scared the pants off him and precipitated a little love duet with the Merry Widow. *Harriet, dear! I'm shot!...* Jeez, what a yellow louse!"

"But, good night, man!" Captain Wallis roared. "Why did you shoot him?"

"Well, you were putting on a show, weren't you?" Spike countered. "And it was flopping, wasn't it? You needed a little drama and you couldn't cut it. Well, I gave it to you. I dragged the show out of the fire with a smashing climax." He took the cigarette out of his mouth and airily flicked off the ash. "Besides," he added nonchalantly, "I supplied a motive for the murder of Abner Holt that even you half-witted coppers could understand."

O'Malley, by this time, was on his feet "The man's insane!" he cried.

"Oh, yeah?" Spike retorted. "Well, I'm just a little smarter than you are. And if I'm insane, what'n'hell does that make you? A Mongolian idiot? No! Just a handsome Irishman with a yen to marry a rich widow. Skipper, drag him off to the can and charge him with the murder of Abner Holt. And if I can't give you enough evidence to send him waltzing at the end of a rope, I'll confess I don't know as much about this case as Jeff Gervin. And he probably doesn't even know who was murdered. Anybody got a drink?"

Willie had a flask which he promptly passed across the footlights. Spike took a long drag, said: "Lousy!"

"I think you'd better explain yourself, Kaylor," Captain Wallis said. "I can hardly arrest a man on a murder charge without more evidence than you've given me."

Spike tossed him the Lüger. "You want evidence? There's your evidence. Break it down and hold the barrel up to the light. What'll you see? I'll tell you. You'll see a smooth bore, no rifling. Mean anything to you? Not a thing! That's because you're only a dumb copper. A nice guy, I'll grant you, but only a dumb copper."

"Quit bragging and get on with your rat-killing," the captain snapped.

"Well, this morning I called on Mr. O'Malley and had a little talk with him. I told him it was just a routine assignment. And while I was there I buzzed him about his collection of guns. I like guns myself. He showed me what he had and I happened to hold the barrel of this Lüger up to the light. It didn't have the silencer on it then. I got that this afternoon from a gunsmith friend of mine. Anyway, the barrel was as smooth as glass. It had no rifling and, funny thing, the caliber looked just a shade too large.

"Well, I didn't say anything, but after I left O'Malley's joint I did a lot of thinking. And I tumbled." Spike took another healthy swig from the flask. "The lay was this. O'Malley had drilled out the barrel of this Lüger and made a smooth bore of it, a bore just large enough to handle a .32 caliber slug.

"He fired a shot from that revolver Katie used into a bag of cotton. He recovered the slug, which then had the distinctive rifling marks of the revolver, and fitted it into a special shell that the Lüger would handle."

Spike lit another cigarette, airily. "No trick to that. My gunsmith friend and I made one this afternoon. Only where O'Malley put enough powder in the cartridge to kill a man, we put in just enough to sting him.... Did it hurt very much, *dearie?*"

O'Malley, ashen-faced and trembling, glared at the cocky Spike and kept his lips clamped shut.

KAYLOR SHRUGGED. "ANYWAY, O'Malley fitted the Lüger with a silencer which he's since ditched. It may turn up and it may not; it doesn't matter anyway. At the crucial moment in the rehearsal, where Abner Holt enters, O'Malley slipped into the wings. When Katie fired, O'Malley let Holt have it in the heart. And with a neat little gat like this, even bored smooth, a good marksman couldn't miss. In the confusion he cached the Lüger and got back on the stage. And that was that.... Well, how does it sound, skipper?"

Captain Wallis looked at O'Malley, and at Harriet Holt, and then again at Spike. "It's all so logical I'm ashamed of myself," he admitted. "But how, Kaylor, did you get the Lüger?"

Spike grinned. "I cased O'Malley's joint till I saw him breeze out to lunch. Then I broke into his apartment and stole the rod."

"You fool!" Harriet Holt screamed suddenly, whirling on Sam O'Malley. "I told you to get rid of that gun."

"Shut up!" O'Malley hissed through clenched teeth.

"But no!" she cried furiously. "You idiotic gun-lover! You had to keep it! You'd get a new barrel! You *loved* that Lüger! And, oh, no! The police would never search your apartment. And even if they did, they'd never examine all your guns. And they wouldn't spot that bored-out barrel if they did. Of all the bigoted, conceited—"

"Shut up, you crazy fool!" O'Malley raged. "Do you want to put your head in the noose?"

Noose! That stopped her. Until she heard that word I don't think she had the slightest inkling of what she was doing. Now her face, red with rage, abruptly went white.

"Jeez, what a dumb Dora!" Willie Blake whispered. "If she hadn't busted out like that, he might have beat the rap."

Captain Wallis stood watching the hysterical widow for a moment or two. Then a faint smile appeared on his lips; he quickly brushed it away with the back of his hand and turned back to Spike.

"You say, Kaylor, that you burglarized this man's apartment?"

"You got me the first time, skipper. I committed first degree burglary. I confess and there's the evidence. And what are you going to do about it?"

"As much as it pains me to admit it, Spike, I'm not going to do a damned thing about it."

Spike gave him a mock salute. Then he turned and looked at us across the footlights.

"How was *it*, gang?" he asked, beaming.

"Well," I said, "nobody has ever called me queer, but I could kiss you, you sawed-off little red-headed bum."

"I'll kiss him for you," Katie said promptly, if a bit hysterically.

"Aw, nuts!" Jeff Gervin snorted. "Let's scram out of here. I got an edition in ten minutes"

"I got an edition, too," I said, hopping up.

We all of us started up the darkened aisle on a dead run. And in some way—I never did find out exactly how—Jeff Gervin got knocked down. He got knocked down, and *out!* They say he didn't come to for half an hour, and missed his edition, and almost got fired. All of which broke nobody's heart.

THE DUCHESS WINS A BET

*Katie Blayne Accepts a Sudden Challenge,
and Snarls Up Cops and Crooks Alike, When
She Tries to Unravel the Twisted Memory
of the Corpse That Defied Oblivion*

1

I SAID: "DON'T talk to him, Duchess. Don't even listen to him. He's a drunk and a bum and a louse."

"I'm two lices," Jeff Gervin grinned. "So what?"

I took Katie's arm. She tried to pull away from me, but I held on. I dragged her across the press room and through the door, while Gervin gave us a very nasty raspberry. Out in the City Hall corridor, I said:

"Now look, Katie. He just hid those arrest slips to get your goat. The more you argue with him, the more he enjoys himself. Let it pass."

"Let it pass!" Katie repeated angrily. "Do you think Miss Tobin let it pass when I got scooped on the arrest of that gangster, Lucky Cabrillo?"

"All of which goes to prove," I said, a bit wearily, because it was an old argument, "that a police beat is no place for newspaper women. I've been telling you that for six months."

"Really! And in the last six months who has broken more big stories off the police beat than any other reporter?"

Well, she had me there. In the months she had been covering police for the *Sun*, Katie Blayne had been making me and Pete Zerker and Jeff Gervin and Willie Blake look like a quartette of not very bright cubs.

"It's ten o'clock, Katie, and we've got to work tomorrow. I'll drive you home."

She gave in with a shrug. She wasn't very good company as I drove out Harrison Street and swung around the lake. My radio was tuned on 27 meters and as we turned up Grand Avenue the speaker came to life.

"Calling Car 31. Calling Car 31. Go to 119 Bayside Terrace. A barking dog. 119 Bayside Terrace. A barking dog. That is all."

I laughed. "That's Pete Freitas and Ed Sullivan. Won't they love chasing down a yapping pooch?"

Katie said crisply: "Turn here, Pinky."

"Huh?"

"Turn!"

I turned. "What's the idea?"

"We're on Bayside Terrace now. Up about two blocks we'll find 119."

"How thrilling. Why the sudden interest in this pooch?"

"Why, I like dogs. Didn't you know?"

"Nuts," I said, but I said it under my breath.

I slowed down, watching the numbers on the curb. A small black sedan whizzed past us, shot in front of my car and pulled up. I drew in behind it. Katie and I hopped out just as Pete Freitas and Ed Sullivan lumbered from the prowl car. There was a street light right over us and the two coppers stared.

"The Duchess!" Pete Freitas growled.

"And Pinky Kane," grumbled Ed Sullivan. "Anybody'd think they was a coupla murders out this way."

"Yeah, and if you don't stop chasin' prowl cars," Pete

The trunk contained a deadly surprise for them

Freitas threatened, "I'll have the chief take that radio off your bus."

You see, Pete and Ed consider themselves pretty important cogs in our law enforcement machine and their present assignment griped them plenty.

We could hear the dog now, yapping steadily, stridently. The barking came from a two-story gray house next door to 119.

A woman, a gray-haired little old woman in black, hurried down the steps of 119, crossed the sidewalk and confronted Officers Sullivan and Freitas with fire in her eye.

"I can't stand it!" she cried hysterically. "It's driving me crazy. It's that Brock dog from across the street. Some way she got into the Felton's basement, next door there, and for a solid hour she's been barking. Brock and Mrs. Felton are partners and—"

"Has that," Sullivan asked slowly and heavily, "got anything to do with this barking dog?"

"No, maybe it hasn't. Only the Feltons have gone to the show—it's bank night—and Brock doesn't seem to be home either. I tried to telephone him. I suppose they went to the show together and left that horrible little yapping dog—"

"Calm yourself, madam," big Ed rumbled. "We police officers have nothing else to do but clam up pooches. Officer Freitas, front and center. Forward march Harumph! Harumph!"

SULLIVAN AND FREITAS, both of them burned to a crisp, started across the lawn and around the darkened gray house. The Duchess lit out after them and I tagged along, a bit burned myself. It seemed to me a lot of people were going to a lot of fuss over a yapping dog.

The basement door at the rear of the bleak gray house stood ajar. Freitas pulled out his flashlight and went in. The rest of us followed. There was nothing in the large cement-floored basement but a big black wardrobe trunk around which capered, barking excitedly, a small fox terrier.

Freitas patted his knee, called: "Here, pup! Here, pup! Nice doggie."

The pup went on barking, without giving Freitas a sign of a tumble. Pete looked around helplessly. I said: "All right, Sullivan. Go into your dance."

Sullivan glared at me, eyed the dog, pulled his long lower lip and said: "Pick him up, Pete. He won't bite us."

"Certainly he won't bite *us*—if *I* pick him up," Pete growled. "How's about you pickin' him up?"

"Well—dogs are a little off my beat. I—"

A step sounded on the walk outside. We turned as a great, broad, thick-chested man filled the doorway. His small, sharp blue eyes blinked in the beam of Pete's flashlight. He said, in a voice heavy and guttural: "That is my dog. My name is Brock. I joost got home from a pigdure show. I am very sorry, gentlemens, if my dog hass been bothering peobul. Usually she does not bark—very mooch. Here, Trixie! Come now to papa."

Trixie pranced about the big black trunk, yipping louder than ever.

"Trixie!" Mr. Brock cried, in a hurt tone.

Trixie ignored her master's voice. Brock finally strode over to the trunk. He poised like a wrestler, waited his opening and finally gathered the pup up in his big arms. The little terrier squirmed, still yapping.

"I take her home now," Brock said. "Something hass excited her. I get her quiet."

"Yes, and see that you keep her quiet!" Ed Sullivan barked.

Brock fled. The two coppers turned toward the door, treading heavily.

"Look here, you two half-wits!" Katie said abruptly.

Sullivan sighed. "Come on, Pete. She ain't speakin' to us."

"I'm speaking to you," the Duchess retorted. "And I'm telling you, you'd better investigate that trunk. That dog hasn't barked at it a whole hour for nothing. If you ask me—"

"Is anybody askin' you?" Pete Freitas snarled.

"Yeah," Sullivan put in. "I'm askin' her—to keep her damned nose out o' other people's business."

But the two coppers had paused. Freitas turned his light back onto the trunk, held it there a dozen seconds, then flashed it around the basement. The beam came to rest on a light switch beside the door. Sullivan snapped it on and Freitas put his torch away.

The two officers walked over to the trunk, stood regarding it thoughtfully, finally walked around it, frowning. The trunk stood on end. I could see it wasn't locked.

Finally, without a word to each other, Freitas took one corner and Sullivan took the other. They yanked. The trunk flew open, the brass corners shrieking on the concrete floor.

The two halves of the trunk swung wide and left a man sitting on the floor, his arms clasped around his doubled-up legs, his head resting against his knees. A man in a gray suit. A *dead* man!

I heard Katie gasp. I caught her arm, said: "Easy, kid!"

And then the corpse, twisted from the ordeal it had suffered, topped over on its side. We could see, now, that the dead man's head was a pulpy mass of dried blood and matted hair. The whole top of it had been beaten in and, from the looks of the waxen face, the glazed eyes, I guessed he had been dead maybe a couple of days.

ED SULLIVAN TOOK a deep breath. "Pete, hit a box and report to Captain Wallis. I'll go upstairs and see if anybody's home in this dump. Felton, the dame next door said their name was. Said they were out. Well, I'll take a look-see. And you two—" He gave Katie and me a glassy stare "—you two keep your mitts off everything. There may be fingerprints—"

"Skip it," Katie said. "We've been around, Pinkie and I."

"Yeah," Sullivan growled. "Around and around, and you come out here. Why? I'd like to know why. A hunch? I doubt it."

"A dog barked, dearie," the Duchess said placidly. "And you know I love dogs."

The cops went out. I saw Katie eye the corpse and then look at her wrist watch. She said soberly:

"It's 10:35. I have an edition in five minutes."

"I have one in ten minutes. So what?"

"So the least we can do is to try to get an identification on this body. Will you do it?"

"No."

"Yes," Katie said flatly. "I'll keep watch at the door."

Well, it was taking a chance, messing around that way. But we, Katie and I, had taken chances before. She stepped outside the door and I ran my hand over the dead man's hip. I felt a wallet, pulled it out, opened it.

In the isinglass window I read: "J.C. Squires, 592 Sunset Boulevard, Los Angeles, Cal."

I copied the name and address on a slip of paper, put the wallet back in the dead man's pocket, and Katie and I got out of there. We found telephones in a drug store three blocks away. We didn't have any facts, of course, but we had enough to hang a story on, a story that would sell plenty of copies of the theater edition.

Driving back, I said to Katie: "That dame said Brock and this guy Felton are partners. Maybe we can pick up something from Brock. Beat the dicks and the other papers. Sullivan and Freitas are too excited—"

"To remember what the old lady said," Katie finished for me.

"Right. We'll put the bee on Mr. Brock."

When he came to the door in answer to our ring, Brock wore a purple dressing gown and looked as big as Man Mountain Dean.

"Miss Blayne of the *Sun*," I said, "and Kane of the *Telegram*. We were across the street with those two cops when you came after your dog."

"*Ja?*" His beady eyes blinked at us. "Und so?"

"We'd like to ask you a few questions about the Feltons."

He started. "They—they haff nod been hurt?"

"Nothing like that, Mr. Brock. May we come in?"

He stood aside, plainly reluctant. Katie and I walked through the short hall and into the small living room. He followed us, nodded us into chairs, said: "Und now, blease?"

"I might as well give it to you straight, Mr. Brock. You saw that trunk in the Feltons' basement. The cops found a body in it. The body of a man by the name of J.C. Squires, from Los Angeles. Know him?"

AT THE WORD Squires I saw Brock's jaw twitch and his eyelids dropped three times, fast. Oh, he knew who Squires was, all right. But get him to admit it?

"I haff never heard uff the men," Brock said calmly.

"You can't recall that your partner, Mr. Felton, ever mentioned such a person in your hearing?"

"Neffer that I recall."

"You have had no business dealings with anybody by that name?"

"Nod any."

"What, may I ask, is your business?"

"We own the Felton-Brock Meat Company. You haff seen our markets, uff course."

"Yes, you have a chain of them. Started up a couple of years ago, didn't you?"

"One year und eight months."

"Made a big success of it, you and Mr. Felton, haven't you?"

Brock shrugged ponderous shoulders. "Maybe we haff. I am a goot bootcher. Mr. Felton is a goot business man. Together, we make a success. *Ja!* So?"

Well, I had a little, but not much. And I had a hunch I'd get no more from Mr. Brock, the "goot bootcher."

"So I guess that will be all," I said.

"Thanks a lot, Mr. Brock."

When we went back across the street to 121 Bayside we found a dozen cars in front of the house and the basement full of men. Dicks, deputy coroners, police photographers, fingerprint experts, reporters, camera men.

I located Spike Kaylor, who covers night police for my paper. "I just phoned the office, Spike. Gave them all I had, including the identification. The Duchess and I, you know, were with the two flatties who found the body. Have the Feltons turned up yet?"

"No. The dame next door says they went to a show. Personally, I got a hunch they've taken a powder. And if they haven't scrammed already, they'll sure take it on the lam when they come back and see all these cars and coppers."

A voice from the doorway said: "If it isn't an intrusion, may I ask what is going on here?"

All activity in the crowded, smoke-filled basement

stopped on the instant. Everyone turned, staring, speech-less for the moment. Captain Wallis, who had been kneel-ing beside the body, straightened slowly.

A MAN AND a woman stood outside the basement door. The man was about thirty-five, tall, even-featured, with steel-gray eyes and black moustache. The woman might have been seven or eight years younger. She was small, blond, more than passably good-looking. She had hold of the man's arm, and she looked frightened.

Captain Wallis broke the tense silence. "You, I presume, are Mr. Fred C. Felton."

"You presume rightly," said Felton. His head did not move but his steel-gray eyes swept back and forth over the basement. I don't believe he saw the corpse, there were so many men standing between him and the doorway.

"I am glad you have come," Captain Wallis said. "Perhaps you can tell me who this man is. Come in, please."

Felton stepped into the basement, his wife clinging to his arm. Her face now was dead white, her blue eyes wide, her lips drawn tight together. I heard Spike Kaylor whis-per: "Guilty as hell!"

"Step aside, men," Captain Wallis ordered.

The men broke to right and left. And there, almost at Felton's feet, was the body of J.C. Squires. The dead man, now, lay on his back, his knees drawn up, his arms still clasped around them, his awful eyes staring.

Felton stepped swiftly in front of his wife, bent slightly, said:

"I never saw the man before in my life."

"Strange," Wallis said calmly. "Strange indeed. We

found him in a trunk right here in your basement. Perhaps your wife might know who he is."

"My wife—" Felton began, and put his arm to hold her behind him.

But Mrs. Felton had moved to one side. She looked down at the dead man. Her eyes widened in horror. She screamed once, briefly, and then dropped in a dead faint.

2

WHEN I REACHED the City Hall press room a few minutes before nine the next morning (I cover day police for the *Telegram*), I found Willie Blake of the *Sentinel* and Pete Zerker of the *Bulletin* already on the job.

The Duchess wasn't there, but in the far corner, his feet propped on a desk, his hat on cock-eyed, a bottle of gin at his elbow, was Jeff Gervin. Now Jeff usually covers night police for the *Sentinel* and should have been in bed at nine o'clock. And Jeff, on this particular morning, had a decided cat-that-swallowed-the-canary look in his small beady eyes.

"Nice murder, eh, Pink?" fat Willie Blake said cheerfully. "Heard you and the Duchess had ringside seats."

"Yeah. What've they done with that guy and his wife?"

"They grilled them until six o'clock this morning and then locked them up," said Lanky Pete Zerker.

"Did they crack?"

"Not any."

"Who is J.C. Squires?"

"A Los Angeles airplane manufacturer."

Something hit me. Squires. Los Angeles. Airplane…. Squires. Los Angeles. Airplane.

"What's wrong, Pink?" Willie Blake asked hastily.

The words kept running through my mind. Squires. Los

Angeles. Airplane. I almost had it when Jeff Gervin said: "Save the effort. The *Sentinel's* got the whole story. The first run's on the street right now. I recognize the guy and the dame as soon as I lamped 'em last night."

"What guy? What dame?" Willie asked blankly.

"Oh, read the *Sentinel*, lug," Jeff Gervin said airily.

I sat down limply, pretty sore at myself for being so slow on the pick-up. "The man's name isn't Felton," I said. "It's Fell. The woman is Mrs. J.C. Squires. She is, or used to be, a stunt flier in the movies, before she married Squires. Remember now?"

Pete Zerker nodded. "It was two years ago. This Squires woman and Fell left Glendale airport one afternoon in her plane. They had dropped hints to several friends that they were tired of it all and that they were going to—"

"I remember!" Willie Blake broke in. "They were going to fly into the setting sun. Drop in the Pacific."

"Yes," I said. "And they were never heard of again "

"Until last night," Pete Zerker concluded, "when they were found living out there on Bayside as Mr. and Mrs. Fred C. Felton. As Jimmy Durante would say, 'Two years have elapsed. He has grown a moustache and he's prospered.'"

"Until the dame's husband located 'em," Willie put in.

"Look!" I said hurriedly. "Do the dicks know who these people really are?"

"I just talked to Captain Wallis," Zerker said. "He isn't wise yet."

"He will be when he sees the *Sentinel's* first edition," Jeff said, as Katie came into the room.

She looked tired this morning. She had no smile for any

of us as she went over to her desk, sat down and took the cover off her typewriter.

"Look Duchess!" Jeff started to ride her. "You seen the *Sentinel* to-day?"

She looked over her shoulder at him, her blue eyes cold and hostile. "It was excellent work on your part, Mr. Gervin. Can we let it go at that, or must we continue inflating your ego indefinitely?"

"Well—" Jeff began.

"AND BY THE way," Katie broke in. "Put this down on your copy paper, just as a matter of record. Mr. Fell and Mrs. Squires had nothing whatever to do with the murder of the woman's husband. How do I know?

"I've just come from an interview with Mrs. Squires. I've been talking to her for the last hour and she told me the whole story. How she was in love with this man Fell. How they flew away from Glendale. How she wrecked the plane in a cañon in the San Bernardino mountains and then burned it and covered the charred wreckage with brush. How they made their way up here, started life over again under the name of Felton, and how the man she loved made good, made a big success of this chain of cut-rate meat markets.

"And she swore to me that she had never seen or heard from her husband from the day she left Glendale until last night when she looked at him lying there on the basement floor."

Jeff Gervin guffawed, pounded his knee, thumped the desk. "And you believed her!" he bellowed.

Katie said flatly: "I believed her."

Jeff was still roaring with laughter. "Duchess, you always

were a sucker for a sob story. That's the trouble with you newspaper dames. You can't keep the omniscient viewpoint. You feel sorry for the Squires wench, who is in a pretty tough spot, so you believe her when she sheds a few tears and tells you she and her paramour are innocent. Duchess, Duchess?"

"You think you're pretty smart, don't you, Jeff?" the Duchess shot back. "All right. You're a betting man. How about this one. I'll bet you a week's pay, your thirty dollars against my forty dollars, that Fell and Mrs. Squires are never convicted."

We all laughed at the look that came over Gervin's face. It burned him plenty that Katie made ten dollars more a week than he did.

"That was a pretty nasty crack, Duchess," he said, glaring at her with tight lips. "The bet is on."

A little later, when Jeff had gone home to bed and the other fellows were upstairs checking the beat, I said to Katie: "Look, kid. That was a foolish bet."

"You think so?" she retorted coldly.

"I think so. You know, Jeff Gervin may be a drunk and a bum, but he's been kicking around a police beat for twenty years and he knows psychology. Just as he said, women reporters are too sentimental. You can't keep the omniscient viewpoint. You—"

"Would you mind, Pinky, keeping the omniscient viewpoint yourself?" the Duchess demanded. "I have a story to write and I'm tired of your prattling."

"Tired—of my— You go to the devil, Katie Blayne!"

LATE THAT AFTERNOON Captain Wallis came into the press room. He looked about ready to drop; I knew he had been up all night grilling Fell and Mrs. Squires, and had been working all day on the case.

"I've just sworn to murder warrants against that pair," he announced, "and they will be arraigned on Thursday. We've traced the trunk. Found they bought it a week ago. We also found the insides, the drawers and hangars, in a clothes closet upstairs, where they had dumped them. And the only fingerprints on the trunk, besides those left by Sullivan and Freitas when they opened it, are the prints of Fells and Mrs. Squires. That's the works, boys. It's enough to hang the both of them."

"And what do they say?" the Duchess asked crisply. "Fells and Mrs. Squires."

"They say they bought the trunk to take a trip to Seattle. They say that the trunk was in the front bedroom, half packed, when they went to the theater last night." Captain Wallis smiled wearily. "They say—they are innocent. But I'm afraid a jury won't see it that way. And, incidentally, the coroner says Squires was first choked to death. Then the killer, Felton of course, beat out his brains."

"He was thorough, anyway," Willie Blake remarked.

"Too thorough." Captain Wallis smiled wanly. "That's all, boys. I'm going home now and get some sleep."

Late that afternoon I was sent over to the morgue to check the identification of a hit-run victim. I met Dr. Jan Steinmetz coming out of the coroner's office. Now Dr. Steinmetz is a private investigator, one of the best. The true detective magazines, which often write up his cases, call him the world's foremost scientific detective. Which may be stretching the truth a little, but not much.

"How's it, Doc?" I said.

"Hello, Kane."

"Got something hot up your sleeve?"

Lanky, thin-faced, shabbily dressed Dr. Steinmetz smiled and said: "Quite so. But not for the *Telegram.*"

"Why not for the *Telegram?*"

"Because I have been retained on this case by the *Sun.*"

"Which case?"

"Why, the Squires murder case, of course." Dr. Steinmetz went his way.

So the *Sun* was putting out good cash to investigate the murder of J.C. Squires. Our fiery little Duchess must certainly have done some fast talking to her close-fisted boss. And, more important from my viewpoint, she must have had something to talk about. I worried about it all the rest of the day.

3

I HAD MY hat on, ready to go home that evening, when the *Telegram's* private office phone rang. Spike Kaylor answered it, said: "Andy wants you," and handed me the phone. Andy is our city editor.

"Yeah," I said into the mouthpiece. "It's six o'clock, and I'm hungry."

"Do I care?" Andy shot back. "Look, Pink. Got a little assignment for you this evening. You know this man Brock, don't you?"

"I buzzed him a bit last night, but I don't know him. Why?"

"Well, the business office is on my neck. Seems Brock is sore because we've given too much space to the Felton-Brock Company angle of this murder. Says it's going to ruin his business. He's been squawking to Carlyle. Threatens to quit advertising in the *Telegram* if we don't square things."

"Square things! Is it our fault his partner commits murder?"

"Anyway, I promised the business office we'd use a little puff story tomorrow. You know, how Brock started from scratch and built up this big chain of markets. You're pretty good at dishing the soft soap, Pink—"

"It's a lie."

"And I want you to see Brock tonight and work up something. Anything to pacify him and get the business office off my neck. That's all, pal. Tally-ho."

I rang Brock's doorbell at nine that evening. He came to the door in his purple dressing gown, took one look at me and said briskly: "I am very busy. Blease excuse me."

He started to close the door but I jammed my foot against it. "Hold it, Mr. Brock. I come with good tidings. The *Telegram* wants a story from you, a real success story. We can use a column."

He stood there a moment, scowling fiercely. Then he pulled open the door, said: "Gum in."

I went to the living room. It was in disorder. Suits, underwear, shoes, various articles of wearing apparel were scattered all over the place. Two or three half packed suitcases lay open on the floor. I paused, looked over my shoulder at the big man. In another part of the house Trixie was barking.

"Scramming, Herr Brock?"

"Vat iss? No! *Ja!* I go to Chicago to hire Franz Noelbaum, the great criminal lawyer. My partner is in trouble. No eggspence we will spare to prove to the vorld his innocence."

"Oh, yeah? Noelbaum comes high."

"We haff blenty money."

"You'll need it, pal."

I WAS RIBBING him and he knew it. He was breathing too fast, his face was too red. His fists, like pink hams, were clenched. And all the time he was smiling, or making a stab at it, anyway.

"Trixie," I said, "must be excited again tonight."

"That tamn dog. She's a nuisance."

"Quite."

He had stopped trying to smile. I was afraid of him. I didn't like the look in his ice-blue eyes. I didn't like those big pink fists. I didn't like his 250 pounds of hard German-trained and German-disciplined body. I knew he could pick me up by the ankles, swing me a few times around his head and splash me against a wall. And I didn't want to be splashed against a wall.

And yet I had to find out an answer to the question: Why does Brock think he's behind the eight ball?

"If you'll quiet that dog," I said, "maybe we can get down to business."

"Business? Vat business?"

Well, that was the pay-off. You see, he'd forgotten already why I was there.

"This puff story I'm going to write. This column of free advertising for the Felton-Brock Company."

"*Ja!*"

"And Trixie?"

"Blease to wait here. I brain that tamn dog."

He opened a door and strode into a disordered bedroom. Trixie was barking at a closed door on the far side of the room. Brock, amazingly light on his feet for so big a man, ran over and gave her a boot that sent her sailing under the bed, where she lay whimpering.

Brock turned, saw me in the doorway of the bedroom. He paused, his sharp cold eyes blinking very fast. From the door at which Trixie had been barking came a muffled rap-rap-rap. Like a high-heeled shoe tapping against a wall!

I felt my stomach turn over. I took half a breath, like a sprinter in that split second before the gun goes off. Then I turned and dove across the living room.

I heard a guttural curse and the pounding of heavy feet. Then I stumbled over an opened suitcase and fell flat on my face. Brock landed on me like a ton, like two tons, of bricks.

He landed on me so hard, from a flying dive, that he rolled completely off me. And left me lying there with every atom of wind knocked out of my lungs, every nerve and muscle in my body completely paralyzed. For a moment that seemed forever, I couldn't move my little finger.

I lay there with my eyes half closed, and watched Brock spring to his feet. He took a step toward me and then paused. I could see him only from the knees down. I saw one of his big feet swing back. Had this big German *kicked out Squires' brains?*

All at once there was life in my aching muscles. I rolled over again and hopped onto my feet.

"You fool!" I yelled. "Don't you know this house is surrounded? One squawk from me and a dozen cops will be in your hair. Take it easy, you sap!"

IT WAS A pretty sick bluff, but it was enough to hold him for a few seconds, enough to cause him to look around in panic to the right and to the left as though he expected to see cops coming from all directions.

I reached behind me, caught up the telephone and yelled: "Help Help! Help!" at the top of my lungs.

I was still yelling when he hit me the first time and knocked me flat. I kept on yelling until his big boot loomed in front of my face and exploded in a shower of red stars and I went out like a light.

When I came to, my head felt like an over-inflated balloon and the sweet-salty taste of blood was in my mouth. I raised up my hands and looked around. Two of the suitcases were gone. And so, thank God, was Brock.

I got up finally on my shaky legs.

Trixie was still whimpering in the bedroom.

I could still hear, faintly, that rap-rap-rap of a high-heeled shoe against a wall.

I found the Duchess on the floor of the bathroom. Her ankles were bound with cord. Her wrists were tied behind her. Her mouth was taped with adhesive. And her blue eyes were wide and frightened.

For a moment I thought of leaving her there for a while, just to teach her a lesson. Then I weakened. After all, she must have heard us scrambling around and me yelling for help. She'd been punished enough—for one night.

I cut the cord on her ankles and wrists and managed, not too adroitly, to get the adhesive off her lips. Then I helped her onto her feet and said: "You're lucky he didn't cave your head in too. What's the score, kid?"

"Where—where is he?" she asked weakly.

"On the lam. Do you tell me the score, or do you tell me the score?"

She swallowed, said haltingly: "Dr. Steinmetz found fingerprints—on Squires' throat. You know, that new—silver nitrate process."

"Brock's prints?"

"We didn't know. All we were sure of—it was somebody who knew—that the Feltons were planning a trip—and had bought that trunk. They haven't many friends. They gave us a list. We've all—the whole staff—been trying to get their prints—by various ruses. I drew Brock. Asked for him. Because—maybe I had a hunch. The coroner, you know, said only a very powerful man—could have crushed a person's skull like that."

"And you came out here and faced that big murdering lunk—alone?"

She dropped her eyes. She swayed a little, put out a hand against the wall to steady herself. I put my arm around her, most impersonally.

"I THOUGHT I was smart, Pinky. Everybody—at the office—thinks I'm smart. I guess—I've got them buffaloed." She laughed a little and then swallowed a sob. "I had some pictures—some shots that Lloyd made last night of the body. I gave them to Brock to look at—to get his prints, you know. And I talked to him—casually—about the case. But I guess—I was too casual. Too damned casual! All at once I could see him getting frightened. I could actually see terror coming into his eyes, Pinky!"

"Yeah. I saw the same thing a while ago."

"Then he seemed to go crazy. I don't remember much after that—till I was here in the bathroom—all trussed up like a Christmas turkey."

Abruptly feet were thumping on the front stairs and in the living room. I heard Katie catch her breath. I felt her start to tremble.

"Easy, kid. Those are cops. Come on."

We went out and found Ed Sullivan and Pete Freitas in the living room.

"Holy cats!" Sullivan exclaimed. "The Duchess!"

"And Pinky Kane!" snorted Pete Freitas.

"Turn over any old board," I said, "and we'll crawl out.

Who knocked out the bridgework, Ed? Who gave you a
pair of shiners, Pete?"

"The same crazy mugg, prob'ly, that mashed your nose
flat," Sullivan muttered.

"Crazy?" I asked.

"Sure. The big punk blew his top," Freitas told us. "Me'n
Ed got the radio flash and pulled up here just as he was
lamming."

"Of course," Ed said. "We didn't know the score. But
soon as he sees us get out of the car he starts to battle.
Thought he could clean me'n Pete. Huh!"

"He didn't do so badly," Katie said, smiling, getting hold
of herself again.

"Well," Sullivan said, "we had to damn near knock his
head off his shoulders to get the bracelets on him. And he
never stopped babbling all the way to headquarters."

Headquarters, I thought! I've evidently been out a long
time.

"Boy, he sure spilled his guts," Freitas said.

"Along what lines, muh franz?" I asked.

"Well, as near as we could piece it together from this
guy's babblin', this Squires found out where his wife and
Fell were. He wanted his wife to come back to him but he
didn't have the courage to go to her or to Fell. So he went
to Brock, thinkin' to have Brock act as a go-between."

"Brock had several meetings with him," Sullivan put in.
"And then, in a burst of inspiration, he conceived his great
plan. He polished off Squires three days ago. Then last
night, when he knew Fell and the Squires dame were at a
show, he planted the corpse in that trunk in the basement.
And left his little dog—"

"That Trixie pooch that's whinin' somewhere around here right now," Freitas broke in.

"To stand watch—and to bark," Sullivan went on.

"But the motive, man!" I yelled. "The motive! Why did Brock want to hang a foul murder on his partner?"

"Because he was sore at Fell. Brock, you understand, was the butcher of the partnership. He got the idea that he was doing all the work and that Fell was only a book-keeper—but a bookkeeper that was taking half the profits of the business. So he figured that if Fell was out of the way, along with the Squires dame, the whole chain of markets would revert to him."

"Nice fellow," I said.

Sullivan poked his tongue through the hole where his front teeth had been. "He packs a nice wallop, anyway."

There were footsteps on the porch and a familiar voice was saying: "…beat her this time, anyway. That *Sun* cub on the police beat is sound asleep. The Duchess is home in bed. And the *Sentinel*, for a change, is—"

And Jeff Gervin stood swaying in the doorway.

"Duchess, you win. Thirty dollars." He groaned, shook his head. "What a lot of gin I could buy for thirty dollars. What's the lay, Pink?"

I started to tell him and after a while I noticed that Katie had disappeared. She was back in a minute, with the whimpering little terrier in her arms. She looked up at me, smiling.

"I'm going to take her home. Didn't I tell you last night I liked dogs?"

THE OLD MAIDS DIE

Katie Blayne, the Duchess, Wins a
Few Bets and Loses Some Sleep in the
Case of the Old Maid Murders

1

THE THREE OF us were playing pinochle in the City Hall
press room when we got the flash; Jeff Gervin, who covers
night police for the *Sun;* Spike Kaylor, who holds down
the beat for my paper, the *Bulletin,* and myself. It was a few
minutes after midnight.

The radio receiver on top of the battery of phone books
blared. "Calling Car 19. Calling Car 19. Go to 748 Myrtle
Street. A woman called for help on her telephone and then
evidently fainted. Step on it, boys."

Sour-faced Jeff Gervin grunted. "Go on and call for help.
See if I care. Deal, will you, Kane?"

I looked at Spike Kaylor, and Spike looked at me. Jeff
Gervin glared, one bushy eyebrow higher than the other,
his thin lips twisted in a sneer.

"Don't be a pair of saps!" Jeff snorted. "If it's a story, the
dicks will bring it in to us. Why borrow trouble? Deal,
will you?"

I stood up and Spike Kaylor followed suit.

"Coming, Jeff?" I asked.

"Me? Leave this nice warm press room to go out on a
phony call like that? On your way, boobs. Scram."

We scrammed.

Prowl Car 19 was drawn up in front of 748 Myrtle Street

"I saw a man, like a big
Negro, leap out the window.
My sister was dead"

and Spike pulled his rattling old flivver in behind it and
we tumbled out.

The big two-story house set well back from the street
on a lot that took in half a block. Spike pushed through a
sagging gate and led the way up a weed-grown gravel path.
From the dim glow of a street lamp half a block away I
could see that the garden had gone to seed and the house
needed paint.

We climbed the creaking, rickety stairs and found the
front door ajar. Spike pushed it open and we walked into
a long bare hallway.

We heard voices coming from a room at the rear and
started down the hall. Spike caught my arm, gasped:

"Good night! Look!"

I swung around, peered through an open door at the

right. All at once I felt sweat coming out on my forehead and the pit of my stomach felt empty and sick.

I was looking into a bedroom, an old-fashioned room with furniture of another day. The bed was longer and wider than they make beds now. The covers and the white counterpane were jumbled.

Half covered by them, with one thin bare leg dragging on the floor, lay an old woman with white hair. The upper part of her face and one side of her head was a bloody pulp.

There was blood on the floor, on the ceiling, on the white bedclothes. It seemed hard to believe that one old woman could have had so much blood in her body.

Beside the bed lay a blood-drenched hammer. A window at the far side of the room was open and the old-fashioned lace curtain was fluttering in the breeze.

"Somebody," Spike said in an awed voice, "played that game for keeps. A thorough job, I calls it. Let's see what the bulls have to say."

We went on down the hall, reached the open door of a large sitting room. On a couch at the far side lay another old woman. She looked exactly like the one in the bedroom.

She was lying motionless, staring at the ceiling with dazed and glassy eyes. Now and then she said dully: "A huge Negro.... A huge Negro!"

Two coppers stood diffidently watching her and looking like they wished they were somewhere else. One of them saw us, glared and demanded: "You guys touch anything in that room?"

We didn't pay any attention to him, for from the open door of the small darkened room at one side came a clear cool voice we knew well—too well!

KATIE BLAYNE, BETTER known as the Duchess, was already on the job. Katie covers day police for the *Sun*. She had no more right to be out on this story than—than *I* had!

"Jeff Gervin?" Katie was saying. "No, he's not out here yet. To be charitable, he's hardly had time. I live only two blocks away, you know, and I happened to have my radio tuned to the police band. So I ran over.

"Here's the lay. These twin spinsters, Malvina and Alva Perkins, live in this old house with their nephew, John Perkins. The nephew is a nightwatchman at the Western Chemical Works, and on the job tonight.

"Alva Perkins was a cripple. She slept in a bedroom on the lower floor. Malvina slept upstairs, where she had a bell that her sister could ring if she wanted anything.

"Somewhere around midnight the bell rang frantically. Malvina rushed downstairs to her sister's room. She was just in time to see a big Negro leap out of the open window and disappear. Alva had been beaten to death with a hammer which lay beside the bed.

"Malvina staggered into the hall, yelled help a couple of times into the telephone and then fainted. She was just coming around when the two officers in the prowl car got here, with me on their heels. The cops sent for Captain Wallis and looked things over perfunctorily.

"They found where the window had been jimmied. There weren't any tracks under it because it opens on a gravel path.... No, there was no attempt at robbery. The Negro probably heard the other sister coming down the stairs and took a powder....

"Yes, the cops have sent out a general pick-up order...."

No, they didn't search the neighborhood. The fellow had plenty of time to make a get-away....

"Yes, that's about all now. I'll turn the story over to Jeff when he gets here—if ever."

Katie came out into the sitting room, nodding to Spike and me.

"Sometime," the red-headed, peppery Mr. Kaylor sputtered, "I hope to come out on a story and not find you ahead of me. Don't you ever sleep?"

"Yeah," said an angry voice from the hall doorway, "and don't you ever mind your own business?" It was Jeff Gervin, winded, red-faced, smelling of gin. "It seems to me that a guy by the name of Gervin is covering night police for the *Sun*. If I'm wrong, wise me."

Katie smiled but didn't say anything. One of the coppers asked: "How'd you get here so pronto, Gervin?"

"I came with Captain Wallis. He and McNaught are in the front room with the body."

The old woman on the couch moaned: "A huge Negro!"

Spike started for the telephone in the little room adjoining. Jeff Gervin began to take the Duchess over the coals for butting in on the story. And the two bulls headed for the front bedroom with me on their heels.

We found Captain Wallis and Mike McNaught, his fingerprint expert, looking over the scene of the murder. The coppers told them Miss Perkins' story.

"This," Wallis said slowly, "is bad. There are twenty thousand Negroes living within a radius of a mile from this house. H-m. Any prints on the hammer, Mike?"

"Not a print," Mike McNaught said.

"Try the window he jimmied. Where's this other sister?"

We had started back along the hall when we heard the door bell buzz. One of the cops answered it. A taxi driver said: "Somebody ring for a cab?"

Katie Blayne came running down the hall. "I did," she called.

I fell in behind her and we went out to the street. Katie paused as the driver threw open the cab door.

"Good night, Pinky. It's been nice to have seen you again."

"Where you bound, Duchess?"

"Home, of course."

"You're calling a cab to drive you two blocks? Tell me another, Katie."

"I'll tell you plenty, Pinky Kane," she retorted sharply. "Dust!"

"Suppose I don't choose to dust?"

Katie glared at me. Then she turned, leaped into the cab and jerked the door shut behind her. I reached for the door handle. The taxi driver said:

"Hold it, pal."

I looked the big gorilla over and decided I wanted none of him.

"Right," I said, and turned toward the house.

2

AS THE CAB rolled off, I ran back to the street and hopped into Spike Kaylor's flivver. Luckily he'd left the ignition key in the lock. I turned it on, revved up the motor and lit out after the cab.

I kept about two blocks behind. The driver, apparently, never knew he was tailed until, half an hour later, we drew up before a large factory building on the other side of the city. For the first time I realized what Katie had on her mind.

We met on the sidewalk beside the cab. The Duchess said with a sigh: "I might have known it. Don't you ever get tired following me around?"

"Not ever. You see, Duchess, I like you. And I want to see that no harm befalls you in your various wanderings over the city after nightfall."

Katie said something that sounded suspiciously like "Nuts!"

The driver leaned out of his cab. "Lady, I can take this lug like Grant took Richmond. How's about it?"

The Duchess shrugged wearily. "Skip it," she said. "How much do I owe you?"

She paid him off, got a receipt to send in with her weekly swindle sheet, and turned again to me.

"I'd appreciate your letting me handle this interview,"

she said. "I have an idea about this murder. You needn't ask what it is, because I'm not putting out anything, but I'd like a free hand when we talk to Perkins. O.K.?"

"I won't say a word, Katie. At least not very many. I have an idea or two myself. Let's go."

We rang a bell at the main entrance of the plant and after a long wait the door was opened by a tall thin man of fifty or thereabouts. He eyed us with disapproval as he asked: "What you want?"

"We're from the *Sun* and the *Telegram,* Mr. Perkins," Katie said. "One of your aunts, Miss Alva, was killed tonight. We want to talk to you about it."

He stood there in the doorway blinking at us, an unpleasant-looking fellow with close-set eyes, thin gray hair and a stoop.

"You can come in, I guess," he said finally.

He led the way along a corridor with offices on either side, down a flight of stairs to the basement and into a small windowless room which was furnished with three or four uncomfortable chairs, a row of lockers against the wall and a deal table. On a one-burner gas plate a pot of coffee was boiling. The whole place reeked of acid fumes.

"You can sit down, I guess," John Perkins said heavily. "What happened to Aunt Alva?"

Katie told him. During the brief recital he poured himself a cup of coffee and drank it black and scalding hot. He asked no questions. He seemed hardly interested.

"We were wondering," Katie said finally, "if you knew anything about the killing of your Aunt Alva?"

He didn't bat an eye at the pointed insinuation. "No," he

said, "I don't guess I know anything about it. A big Negro you say? No, I don't know any big Negroes."

Katie's eyes glittered. "By the way, Mr. Perkins, have you been the sole support of your two aunts?"

"Me? I should guess not." His voice, now, was bitter. "Them two old women are worth a hundred thousand dollars, more or less." He poured himself another cup of coffee, added heavily: "My father left it to them in trust. When they die, I get it."

"And in the meantime, you're working as a night watchman at fifty or sixty dollars a month?" Katie remarked.

"Forty-five," the drab Mr. Perkins corrected.

"And you're not the least bit resentful?" Katie pursued.

He looked her coldly in the eye; his mouth was grim. "If you think I'm not, you're crazy!" he snapped. And then he chuckled harshly. "I see what you're getting at, I guess. Well, you're wrong. Didn't Aunt Malvina say it was a Negro killed Aunt Alva?"

"That's what she said," Katie admitted. "But she might have made a mistake."

"Aunt Malvina," John Perkins declared, "doesn't make mistakes. However, I got something here I ought to show you, just in case you and the police get any foolish ideas about me."

We followed him upstairs. He stopped at a time clock near the outer door, took a card from the big rack, handed it to Katie. I peered over her shoulder.

It was Perkins' card. The last stamp on it showed the date and the time: 1:01 a.m. The previous stamp read: 11:59 p.m.

"I have to ring in, you see, every hour," John Perkins explained.

I looked at the clock. I knew the type. I had punched one like it in a warehouse where I worked before I broke into the newspaper racket. Another fellow and I had tried to set it back when we got to work late one day. We'd discovered it couldn't be rigged.

"You told me," Perkins said, "that Aunt Alva was killed about midnight. I rung in here at one minute to twelve. It takes me a half hour to drive home. You can draw your own conclusions, I guess."

KATIE STARED AT him for a long moment before she asked quietly: "What's the current rate in the Black Belt for a job like that?"

John Perkins grinned. "A hundred dollars, I understand." Then his jaw set and all at once his ice-blue eyes were hard. "I'm not sorry my aunt is dead. She was an old harridan and she got what's been coming to her for a long time. I'm only sorry the fellow didn't kill Aunt Malvina too. Now I guess that's about all I got to say. You people can get the hell out of here."

Which we did.

Just before I left Katie at her home she said abstractedly:

"I talked to Malvina Perkins. She's a mean old woman. And she's a little queer. Perhaps she's even crazy. I wonder—?"

"You wonder if maybe Malvina killed her sister and cooked up the story about the Negro?"

The Duchess merely said, "Good night, Pinky. Pleasant dreams."

I drove off laughing to myself. That was Katie. If her first hunch proved to be a dud, she lost no time in giving birth to another. Katie Blayne can produce hunches faster than a cigarette machine turns out coffin nails.

When I got back to the City Hall I found Jeff Gervin and Spike Kaylor having a drink in the press room.

"I'll have one of those," I said.

"Yes, and I'll have the key to my car," Spike shot back. "What was the brilliant idea?"

"I was riding herd on the Duchess. We had a talk with John Perkins. We discovered that those two old maids are plenty wealthy and Perkins is their heir. The dough was left to them by Perkins' father, and Perkins is pretty bitter about it. But—Perkins' time card was punched at one minute to twelve and it's a half hour's run from that factory to his home."

Jeff Gervin grunted. "You and the Duchess get the damnedest ideas. The guy who knocked off the old dame is now cooling in the can. Name of Jim Brown."

I choked on Jeff's bourbon, reached for the water.

"They picked up this Jim Brown just after you ran off with my car," Spike explained. "He was only three blocks away. A big Negro, dead drunk, with a cut on his head and blood all over his hands. He was staggering along the street talking to himself."

"Lyle and Allen spotted him," Jeff took up the story. "They dragged him into their prowl car, took him in to the Perkins dame, and she went into hysterics."

"Identified him on the spot," Spike concluded.

"So that's that," Jeff said. "Nice work, I calls it. Have another drink?"

I had another drink and went home.

The next day about noon I saw Katie Blayne talking to John Forsythe in the anteroom of the Detective Bureau. Forsythe is one of our better criminal lawyers, a fellow who won't look at a case unless important money is involved, but a right guy at that.

A little later, when Forsythe dropped into the press room, I jumped him.

"You're not, by any chance, going to defend this Negro, are you?"

"I am," Forsythe said flatly.

The room at the moment happened to be crowded with a few reporters and more than a few press room habitués: bail bond brokers, politicians, coppers off duty and other riff-raff that is constantly getting in our hair. Everybody looked at the tall, immaculate, gray-haired, lean-faced lawyer.

"What's the answer to that one?" fat, moon-faced Willie Blake of the *Sentinel* demanded. "I mean, who's putting up the dough?"

"The *Sun*," Katie Blayne declared, "is putting up the dough."

"How come?" I asked.

"Miss Blayne," said Forsythe, "has convinced her publisher that the boy is innocent. And I am forced to agree."

"Who wouldn't agree," Willie grinned, "for a couple of G's?"

"What makes you think this Jim Brown is innocent?" lanky lantern-jawed Pete Zerker of the *Bulletin* asked reasonably. "How about the identification? How about the blood all over him?"

"The old lady could be mistaken in identifying him," Forsythe pointed out. "And the blood was Jim Brown's own. He had fallen down, you know, and had cut his head."

"Sure," I said. "He fell down when he hopped out that window."

"Furthermore," the attorney went on coolly, "the police found no fingerprints on the lethal weapon. Now do you really believe that a drunken Negro boy, a young fellow who is not very bright anyhow, would have the foresight to wear gloves?"

"The prints were probably smeared," Willie Blake suggested.

"There were no prints," Forsythe stated flatly, "smeared or otherwise."

And that was that—for a while.

3

JIM BROWN WAS arraigned on a charge of first-degree murder the next day and his preliminary hearing was set for a morning three weeks hence.

A little before nine on the morning of the preliminary, Katie Blayne showed up at the press room with a confident smile and a breezy, "Good morning."

"I have here," she announced to Pete Zerker and Willie Blake and me, "a hundred dollars which says that the case against Jim Brown will be dismissed before noon to-day. You may have all or any part of it."

"You're pretty confident, Duchess," Pete growled.

"You must be nuts," Willie said. "With the old dame identifying him he's a cinch to be bound over to the superior court. If I were you, Duchess, I wouldn't risk my money on a crazy bet like that."

"You let me worry about my money," Katie shot back. "How much would you like, Willie?"

Willie gulped, shrugged, said: "I'll take a fin."

"Pinky?"

"I'll take ten," I said without enthusiasm.

"Pete?"

"I'll take vanilla," Zerker snapped.

At ten o'clock we were all at the press table in the justice court. The D.A. and a couple of his staff came in, looking blustery and important. Then John Forsythe wandered down the aisle, looking very cool and confident, nodding to his friends among the spectators and at the press table.

The judge arrived and finally the bailiff came trailing in with the prisoner, a big, poorly dressed, frightened-looking colored boy who sat down awkwardly beside John Forsythe.

The hearing got under way with the D.A. making a brief statement of the case and calling Miss Malvina Perkins to the stand. The thin, tall old lady bustled over to the witness chair and sat down. Her lips were thin and pressed tightly against her teeth. Her eyes were glittering, too bright. A shrewish, vindictive, bitter old woman, and could you blame her?

After she was sworn, the district attorney rose and with gentle deference began his examination.

"Miss Perkins, please tell the judge what happened in your home on the night of June fourteenth."

"I was in my room on the upper floor," the spinster began in a shrill voice. "It was a few minutes before midnight. I heard my sister ring for me. Frantically. She was an invalid and sleeping on the lower floor. I ran downstairs and into her room. I saw a man, a big Negro, run across the room and leap out the window. My sister was dead, beaten to death."

The D.A. slowly nodded. "Did you see this man's face?" he asked.

"I did."

"Clearly?"

"Clearly."

"Could you identify him if you saw him again?"

"I certainly could."

"Do you see him in this room?"

"Yes!" the old woman hissed.

"Please point him out to the court."

Miss Perkins leveled a skinny finger at the black boy beside John Forsythe.

"That's him!" she screamed. "That's the monster that killed my poor crippled sister."

"Are you absolutely positive, Miss Perkins?" the D.A. persisted gently.

"Certainly I'm positive!" the old lady shot back. "Do you think I could ever forget his horrible face?"

Everybody stared at the prisoner. His face wasn't horrible at all. It was just the face of a bewildered kid.

John Forsythe was whispering to him. The black boy was nodding his head.

Abruptly I felt an electric tension in the room. I forgot to listen to the D.A., to Miss Perkins' testimony.

I watched John Forsythe and the black boy. The kid was grinning now. Forsythe whispered to him again and he wiped the grin away with the back of his hand.

I glanced at Katie. She, too, was watching Forsythe and the prisoner. And there was something in her blue eyes that told me I had lost ten dollars.

She leaned toward me and whispered: "Cover up your ears, Pinky. The dynamite is going off in just a second. See? Mr. Forsythe is lighting the fuse."

I looked around at Forsythe. He was standing now, placidly buttoning the lower button of his neat double-breasted coat.

"If it please, Your Honor," he said.

THE DISTRICT ATTORNEY swung around, glaring. "You may have the witness in due time," he snapped. "Until I am finished with her—"

"If the court pleases," Forsythe broke in. "I believe a most regrettable error has been made."

"Error?" The judge glared down over the rims of his spectacles. "What manner of error, Mr. Forsythe?"

"Your bailiff has brought in the wrong prisoner."

"The—the *which?*" the district attorney gasped.

"I'm sure it was all a misunderstanding, Your Honor," Forsythe went on smoothly. "But this young man here is one Ed Higgins, who has just finished serving a sixty-day sentence for assault and battery. On the night Miss Alva Perkins was murdered, Ed Higgins was in jail."

The judge leaned forward, staring at the black boy. "I remember. I sentenced him myself." He swung on the bailiff. "Where is Jim Brown?"

The bailiff winced. "I guess, Your Honor, he's still in the city prison. I—I—"

The judge silenced him with a wave of his hand.

I whispered to Katie: "What did it cost Forsythe to have the wrong prisoner brought in?"

"S-s-s-sh!"

The judge had turned on the white-faced Miss Perkins. "Madame, you are an old woman. And I recall an old song to the effect that all colored people look alike. I could point out that your testimony might have sent an innocent man to the gallows, but I don't think it is necessary. Mr. Forsythe, I don't know how you engineered this coup and I am not going to inquire. The end, certainly, justified the means. Do I hear a motion requesting the case against Jim Brown be dismissed?"

"I make such a motion, Your Honor," Forsythe smiled.

The judge looked over at the D.A. We all looked at the D.A. And saw that that smug gentleman had collapsed in his chair.

"Any objection?" the judge asked.

"No," the district attorney said sadly. "No objection."

The gavel banged. "Case dismissed!"

Back in the press room Katie didn't rub it in—much. She took my ten-spot and Willie's five.

"Thank you kindly, gentlemen," she said. "I'm only sorry it wasn't more."

"If it had been any more," I grumbled, "I wouldn't eat until next pay day. Look here, people. How do you figure that Miss Perkins?"

"Ask me a tough one," Willie Blake said. "That dame deliberately identified the first suspect the cops dragged in. Why? Because she polished off her sister herself. Right, Pete?"

"Wrong, Willie," the *Bulletin's* reporter came back. "I figure the poor old woman was so overcome with grief and hysteria and a very natural vindictiveness that she really thought Jim Brown was the man she'd seen jumping out the window."

"Well, Duchess?" I asked. "What's your theory?"

"My theory," said Katie, "is not for publication."

"Getting exclusive, huh?" Pete Zerker jeered.

"I have always been exclusive," said the Duchess with a toss of her shapely blond head.

In the days that followed the police went on looking for

a big Negro whom Miss Perkins could positively identify, the gang in the press room went on with its routine run of crimes and accidents, and the Duchess went on being mysterious.

And I was worried. I think about as much of Katie Blayne as I do of my right eye, despite the fact that she treats me like she'd treat a nice soft rug—just something pleasant to walk upon.

I was worried because I know Katie, know her every mood. She was getting ready to put something over on us. And when Katie gets that watch-me-pull-a-fast-one look in her big blue eyes, I get ready to drag her out of trouble by the hair of her very lovely head. Of course, there have been occasions when she turned the tables and dragged me out of trouble, but we needn't go into that.

I took Katie out occasionally during these weeks and one night, starting home from a movie in my car, we picked up a two-alarm on the police broadcast.

"Want to go?" I asked, thumbing through my list of stations.

"Did you ever know me to pass up a fire? Where is it?"

"Fourth and Polk."

"Let's get under way."

4

FOURTH AND POLK is in the factory district. It took us twenty minutes to get there. We watched a rattan factory go up in smoke and it was about midnight when we ran into Spike Kaylor and Jeff Gervin.

"Hey, you lugs," Jeff called. "How's about a ride back to the Hall?"

I looked at the Duchess. Though now they worked on the same paper, Katie and Jeff, as you may have guessed, were like a couple of strange bulldogs.

"It's all right with me," she shrugged. "Jeff, did you get the name of that fireman who had his hand cut?"

"Did I get—Listen, Duchess! Are you telling me—"

"Skip it. Both of you," I ordered. "Here's the car. Get in, you two."

Jeff and Spike got into the rear seat. As I started off I switched on the radio. It warmed up, the hum died and we heard:

"… Car 19. Calling Car 19. Go to 748 Myrtle Street. That's the house where Alva Perkins was murdered two months ago. A citizen just phoned he saw a Negro leaving the house. Step on it, boys."

Spike whistled. "Boy, they got the other old maid! Sure as shootin' they—"

"Oh, Pinky, Pinky!" Katie Blayne cried in a voice choked

with pain and horror. "Something has gone wrong! Something terrible has happened!"

I shot a quick look at her. Her face was dead white. Her mouth was slack, her lips trembling. There was terror in her eyes.

"That poor old woman!" she groaned, twisting her hands. "That poor old woman!"

"Step on it, mugg!" Jeff Gervin snapped. "Get us out there to 748 Myrtle. Open her up, damn it! Won't this crate do better than forty?"

Katie's fingers were suddenly biting into my arm.

"No, no, no!" she cried. "The Western Chemical Works! Quick! Turn around!"

I smelled the whiskey on Jeff's breath as he leaned forward and yelled into my ear.

"To hell with that! Keep going, Kane!"

"Please, Pinky," the Duchess begged. "Please do as I ask you. I know what I'm doing. I know I'm right."

"Take us out to Myrtle Street, I tell you," Jeff ordered angrily.

"I'll take you where I damn well please," I retorted. "If you want out, hop when I swing this corner."

I swung the corner and he didn't hop. We were, then, only half a mile from the Western Chemical plant and I made it in thirty seconds. I drove the car around to the rear of the four-story building, slammed on the brakes and cut the motor.

"Well, we're here, Duchess," I said. "Now what?"

"Come on," she called, and was out of the car.

We trailed her around to the front of the building and

she opened the door with a key she pulled out of her handbag. We went in behind her and she closed the door.

"Where'd you get the key?" I asked.

"The plant manager."

She walked straight down the hall to the time clock.
There was a card in the slot. Katie took it out and I saw it
was John Perkins' card and was stamped 12:01 a.m.

And then I saw several other things. One was a cheap
alarm clock standing on top of the big time clock. The
alarm bell had been removed and a spring device attached
to the clapper. Hanging from the lever at the side of the
time clock, at the end of a two-foot rope, was a window
weight.

"He set the alarm clock at midnight," Katie said breathlessly. "When it went off, that spring tripped the window
weight."

"And the weight fell about four feet," I said, "and jerked
the lever which stamped Perkins' card. Neat."

"All of which," Jeff Gervin grumbled, "adds up to what?"

Jeff was a bit drunk and slow on the pick-up. Nobody
answered him.

"Maybe," I suggested half-heartedly, "he just rigged it to
get himself a couple of hours sleep. We could look, anyway."

We started down the dim corridor to the stairway.

"This is awful," Katie said, with a catch in her voice.
"Some one has made a horrible mistake."

"Hold it, guys!"

It was Spike Kaylor. I checked myself, startled at the
tension in Spike's voice. He had dropped to his knees on
the stained and rather dirty concrete floor. He rubbed a

dark damp spot with his finger, held the finger close to his eyes.

"Blood," he said calmly.

A LITTLE CHILL of apprehension and bewilderment swept down my spine. All at once I didn't like this great dimly lighted chemical plant with its strange and acrid smells.

Spike was crawling along the floor on all fours.

"More of it," he said. "It's smeared. Like something was dragged over it."

"The something," I said, "being a body." I looked sharply at Katie. She was biting her lower lip. There was horror in her fine eyes. "Whose, Duchess" I asked.

"The man who has been tailing Perkins for nearly two months," she said heavily. Then she started forward. "Hurry! He might not be dead yet."

We all ran down the corridor to the stairway which led to the basement. Katie got there first, cried: "Good grief! Look!"

The wide stairway was jammed almost solid with broken crates and boxes, pasteboard cartons and excelsior.

"One match," Spike remarked, "and this dump would go up like a skyrocket."

Katie hurled aside a smashed crate and started down the stairs. The rest of us turned to and in three or four minutes we cleared enough of a path to worm our way into the basement. There was a light burning in the watchman's little room.

On the floor, sprawled grotesquely just as it had been dumped, lay the body of a man in a blue serge suit. His hat was gone. The top of his bald head was red and pulpy. We knew, by the set and tortured look on his face, by the glassy stare in his eyes, that he was dead.

"You know him, Katie?" I asked.

"Yes. He's a private detective by the name of Jones. My paper hired him." She wrung her hands. "Oh, if only Captain Wallis had listened to me! I knew, I *knew*, that the first murder was planned! And there was only one man who had anything to gain by killing those old maids.

"But Captain Wallis only laughed at me," Katie rushed on hysterically. "Said there was no evidence against Perkins. Said it was just another one of my pipe-dreams. So the *Sun* hired Jones to keep watch on Perkins. And Perkins must have found out he was being watched, and sneaked up on this poor man and—and killed him brutally."

Katie buried her face in her trembling hands.

Spike said: "And then Perkins rushed home and killed his other aunt. He figured to get back here, recover his time card for an alibi and then fire the joint. A neat plan. The dicks picking up that Negro kid right after the first murder was just coincidence. Only—"

"Malvina swore she saw a Negro leap out of her sister's window," I pointed out.

"Of course!" Katie exclaimed. "That was all part of his plan. With the police believing the first old maid was killed by a Negro, they'd naturally suppose that the other had been killed by the same man."

"Yes, but—" I began.

"S-s-s-sh!" Jeff Gervin hissed. "You guys hear that?"

"Hear what?" I whispered. If I heard anything, it was my own knees knocking together.

"Somebody," Jeff rasped, "just shut the front door!"

My heart came up in my throat as I thought of that pile of tinder blocking the stairway.

"Let's go, gang!" I yelled.

I kicked a box out of the way and shoved the Duchess up two steps. Then, for some reason, I looked up.

And peering down at us over the pile of tinder that clogged the stairway was a big black Negro!

No, not a Negro! Just John Perkins, his coat thick with padding, his thin face coated with burnt cork!

John Perkins' head and shoulders disappeared. Then I heard his feet strike the concrete floor three times as he hurled his weight against the pile of broken crates and boxes which filled the stair well.

"Look out!" Spike yelled.

I jerked Katie backward off the steps, lost my balance and fell against Spike and Jeff.

As I scrambled to my feet I saw that the stair well was clogged solidly.

"Look, you lugs!" Jeff Gervin sputtered. "We gotta get out of here!"

"Are you telling me?" Spike snorted. "Where does this corridor lead to?"

5

IT LED, AS we could readily see, to a brick wall at one end
and to a steel fire door at the other. It was a cinch the fire
door was bolted, but it was our only chance of getting out
of the trap we'd blundered into.

I started toward it, heard at that instant the splash of
liquid on the pile of tinder in the stair well.

"Gasoline!" Jeff Gervin screamed. "Get back! Get back!"

In an instant the stairway was a crackling, roaring mass
of flame. I ran to the steel door at one end of the corridor.

I pounded it, kicked it, hurled my weight against it. It
was as solid as Gibraltar.

Catching Katie's hand, I raced her down the hall, past
the appalling heat of the stairway and into the watchman's
little room. Spike and Jeff came after us.

"Slam that door!" I ordered. "The air in here is O.K.
We've got to keep it that way!"

"Yes," Spike said heavily, "and when those big vats of
acid out in the main plant let go. What then? I ask you,
what then?"

Katie had picked up a newspaper on the table and
walked over to the door.

"Help me, Pinky," she said quietly. "You know how the
miners do when they're trapped. We'll plug up all the
cracks around the door. If we can keep out the monoxide

and the acid fumes, the air in here will keep us alive for hours.

"Hours, hell!" Jeff growled bitterly. "The alarm probably isn't even in yet. Another five minutes and the whole inside of this joint will be gutted. I've seen chemical plants go up before."

"Skip it, Jeff!" I snapped, and knelt beside the Duchess and started to plug the cracks around the door.

Katie said in an undertone: "I'm sorry I got you into this, Pinky."

I put my arm around her and drew her close. She put her head against me and I felt a tear drop on my hand.

"Forget it, kid," I said. "You didn't get me into this. We came into it together, just like I wanted to do a lot of things."

She looked up at me. Her face was deathly pale; her eyes were shining.

"Such as?" she asked.

"Such as get married. And go places, and see people, and do things. Together. You and me."

She nodded slowly. "If we'd been married, months ago when you first asked me, I probably wouldn't have been working now. And I wouldn't have blundered into this mess. And you—"

Spike Kaylor abruptly shoved me aside, put his ear to the door. I could hear, very faintly, shouts and a familiar hissing sound as tons of water poured on flames.

"Can you tie it?" Spike yelled jubilantly. "The brave fire laddies are with us. Now how in Sam Hill did they get on the job without us hearing a single siren?"

"Cinch!" Jeff Gervin growled. "The apparatus was

coming by here on its way back from the wicker works fire. They just pulled up, hooked on their hoses and—"

Katie had risen to her feet. "And we'll be out of here in a few minutes." She looked at me, smiled a bit sheepishly. "Pinky, do you suppose everybody gets sentimental when they're in a tight spot?"

I groaned. What we'd said hadn't seemed sentimental to me at all.

In ten minutes we were out of it, standing around a body the fireman had carried to the sidewalk.

"Who is he, Kane? What do you make of it?" Battalion Chief Murphy asked me. "We found him in the hallway at the head of the stairs."

"He's the bird who touched it off. He spilled too much gasoline around, I guess, and when it blew it knocked him over. Now I've got to hit for a telephone."

The four of us, Katie and Jeff and Spike and I, climbed into my car. We found telephones in an all-night drug store eight or ten blocks away, and phoned our stories.

KATIE AND I came out of our booths at the same time. "You had it doped exactly right, Katie," I said. "Perkins had been home and killed his other aunt. How did you do it?"

Katie shrugged. "It wasn't hard. The police didn't find a sign of a fingerprint on the push button beside Miss Perkins' bed. Proving—"

"That the old woman didn't ring for help," I said quickly. "But someone who knew about that button did. Someone who was wearing gloves. John Perkins, of course."

"And Captain Wallis," Katie said bitterly, "laughed at me."

"Don't feel badly, Katie. There was no evidence against

Perkins. They couldn't watch him forever, and sooner or later he'd have slipped away and killed Malvina. Let's forget it. Let's forget everything. Everything except what we said while we were down there waiting to go up in smoke. Look! Don't you think it would be a good idea to marry me and get out of this rotten newspaper racket?"

She smiled at me, shook her head, said: "No. No, Pinky."

"Is that final?" I demanded.

"Well—practically final."

"Any time," Jeff Gervin growled. "Any time you two love-birds get through cooing, I'd like to get back to the Hall and kill this pint I just bought. Fires give me a thirst."

Jeff Gervin gives *me* a pain in the neck.

THE MYSTERY OF THE BARRIO SNATCH

*Reporters Katie Blayne and Pinky
Kane Prove the Power of the Press Is
Sometimes Greater Than the Law*

1

I GOT MY first intimation of the Barrio kidnaping mystery when I walked into the Detective Bureau early one evening to glance over the arrest slips. Only I didn't realize then there was any mystery about it. I thought it was just another snatch.

The sergeant on duty had stepped out for a minute and the big room was deserted. The door to Captain Bodie Wallis's private office was open a few inches, however, and I heard a man's voice; high-pitched, almost hysterical:

"A hundred thousand dollars, Captain! Why, I could not raise ten thousand."

My first thought was of bail bonds. Somebody held in a hundred G's bail. Well, that's a lot of bail, even if the dollar is worth only sixty cents. Then the Captain's voice brought me up like a clip on the chin.

"But where did this snatch mob get the idea you were so lousy with kale?"

Snatch mob! Did my ears prick up!

"Pardon, Captain?" The other man's voice had a strong Spanish accent.

"I said, Dr. Barrio, why would these kidnapers choose your daughter to hold for a hundred-thousand dollars? These mobs don't grab any girl who happens to wander along the street. When they make a snatch, they know what they're doing. They know to the last red cent how much cash a family can raise."

"That I cannot understand, except—well, a few years ago I was rated a wealthy man, perhaps a millionaire. But with the slump in coffee prices—"

"I get it," Wallis interrupted. "Let me see that ransom note again."

Well, I got out of there. My brain was reeling and I wanted a minute or two to collect my thoughts before I let anybody discover I'd overheard that conversation. I went out the door so fast I almost bowled over Katie Blayne, who covers police for the *Sun,* my rival sheet.

Katie caught her balance and glared at me. "If you had brains enough to get into college, Pinky Kane, you'd make a wonderful fullback."

I gripped her arm. "Look, kid! Don't go in there!"

"Says Mr. Kane?"

The Duchess can be plenty nasty when some one rubs her the wrong way, or tries to push her on her ear.

"Please, Katie! Please do as I tell you for once. Don't go in there."

"And why not! Has the *Sun* suddenly been barred from this office—or has one of the stenographers from the auditor's department strolled off the reservation? I always have wanted to catch Captain Wallis in a compromising—"

"Skip it, kid!" I pleaded. "Take a stroll down the corridor with me."

"And?"

"I'll tell you everything. I'll shoot the works."

AT THAT INSTANT the door of the Captain's private office opened and a slight, dark, animated man of about fifty

"Okay, Doc. Let's have the money"

stepped out, closed the door and hurried off. Katie gave me a quick look and then her fine blue eyes followed the little man until he disappeared around the turn of the corridor.

"Oke, Pinky," she said calmly, and slipped out of my grasp with a movement she must have learned from Strangler Lewis. "Are you putting out, or am I asking Captain Wallis why Dr. Barrio was calling on him?"

"You know the little guy?" I asked quickly.

"Certainly I know him. Andreo Barrio. Doctor of Laws, or Philosophy, or some such thing from the University of Guatemala. An authority on the Mayas. Loves to talk about them to the women's club. Once a big-shot coffee importer. Worth a million a few years ago. Went broke when coffee hit bottom." She waited a moment. "Spill it, Pinky."

Well, I'd put myself on the spot and had to come clean. "Dr. Barrio's daughter," I said in an undertone, "has been snatched and held for a hundred grand ransom."

The Duchess whistled. "Carlotta Barrio!"

"You know her too?"

"Met her a couple of times. She's about twenty. A spoiled brat with a high handshake and a voice she thinks is better than Grace Moore's." She whistled again, softly. "Well! Isn't this something!"

"It's a lot of things, Katie. It's a tough break for the doctor and his daughter. It's a damned outrage. It's a blot on American civilization. And it's news, Duchess. It's *news!* It's the biggest story that has hit this burg since the big wind of '66. *But*—I have a strong hunch it'll be some time before we can break it."

I recounted the conversation I'd inadvertently overheard. "This is only a hunch, but I'm offering five to four there was a 'no publicity' clause in that ransom note, and Captain Wallis is just dumb enough, or smart enough, to say 'no soap!'"

"What of it?" Katie retorted. "We have the tip, haven't we? And we'll get the story, won't we? And if we want to break it, let him try and stop us."

"Yes, but suppose your daughter's life was in danger? Suppose—"

"Suppose we have a talk with the Captain."

"Now take it easy," I pleaded. "Let's do this right. Let's not show our ace cards. If Wallis isn't putting out, we'll soft pedal and save the story for the *Sun* and the *Telegram*. Katie, we'll have it exclusive! And your A.P. and my U.P. will scoop the world!"

"I'm not interested in the world," the Duchess said promptly, "but I'd certainly like to put one over on those high-binders in the press room, Let's go."

We knocked on the Captain's private door. He called and we went in. Bodie Wallis is a scholarly-looking man of fifty-five, with sparse sandy hair, thin pink cheeks and penetrating ice-blue eyes.

"Howzit, Skipper?" I said. "I and the Duchess—Miss Blayne to you—are checking the gate. Anything popping or about to pop?"

Captain Wallis was lighting a cigar; he watched us through the smoke that billowed from his thin lips.

"Not a thing, Kane. The town is dead." He smiled wryly. "The way I like it to be."

"Haven't you something we could fluff into a story?" Katie asked. "Something hot enough to carry a banner in our first editions?"

"I haven't anything hot enough to melt ice."

"Oh, yes?" I looked at him hard. "Well, have it your own way, Skipper."

HE STOOD UP slowly, laid his cigar on the charred corner of his desk. His eyes as bleak as a December sky, he asked slowly: "Just what, Kane, was the meaning of that crack?"

"You're a detective, Skipper. Figure it out. Let's scram, Duchess."

Katie and I went out into the corridor. On our way down

the stairs to the press room, I said: "Well, what'll we do about this? Are we breaking the story tonight, or are we letting Wallis give us the run-around?"

"We're breaking the story tonight. But first we'll have to check it and that won't be easy. If I know my Dr. Barrio, he'll deny everything."

"And if we do get him to admit something, and break it, we may endanger the life of his daughter."

"You're not softening up on me, are you?" the Duchess demanded scornfully.

"No, but—"

"Pass it."

"All right, I'll pass it. What do you want to do next? I'm merely asking," I added sarcastically, "now that you've taken over my story."

She smiled then. "You didn't have to tell me," she pointed out.

"No, but I had to keep you out of that room. If you'd got wind of the snatch, then Wallis would have had to give it to everybody. And If I couldn't get it exclusive for the *Tele-gram*, I'd rather share it with you alone than with the whole gang. Now I suggest we give Barrio time to get home and then go out there, wherever he lives, and put it up to him. And I'm not going to tip my office till after I talk to Barrio."

"Oke. I won't tip mine either." She held out her hand and I took it. She said, smiling: "For once, Pinky Kane, let's play fair with each other."

"That," I said, "might be a lot of fun. We've never tried it, have we?"

For six months, ever since the Duchess came over to

cover police for the *Sun,* catch-as-catch-can rules had been invoked in the press room.

At nine o'clock that evening, Katie and I got out of my car in front of the Barrio home, a large two-story house on the edge of town. It set well back from the street in the center of several acres of garden. The garden, even in the poor light from a single street light looked run down. The house, I could see, needed paint. Half a dozen cars drawn up in the driveway.

"Must be a meeting of the Sons of Latin-America, or something," I said.

"At guessing, Pinky, I suspect you're pretty good."

"Meaning?"

"These Latin-Americans stick together. If Dr. Barrio hasn't a hundred thousand dollars in cash, he has plenty of wealthy friends. Let's walk in as though we were invited."

WE PLODDED UP the gravelled driveway, mounted the stairs rang the bell. A woman, about forty, very blonde and hard of eye, opened the door a few inches. From what I could see of her, she didn't look like a maid, nor like I expected Mrs. Barrio to look.

"We'd like to see Dr. Barrio," I announced.

She opened the door a little wider, so that the light fell on us. She looked us over with those hard, appraising eyes and said with finality:

"Dr. Barrio can't see anyone."

As she started to close the door. I stuck my foot out and jammed it open, "Just a moment, please."

The woman was suddenly snarling as she shouted: "Get out! Get out or I'll call the police."

"The police, madam, are already here."

I took out my press badge and flashed it from the palm of my hand and then stuck it back in my pocket. She didn't know whether I was a deputy, a G-man or a correspondence school detective.

"We want to see Dr. Barrio immediately. Do you let us in, or do we get a warrant?"

She looked like she wanted to fly at my throat, but she opened the door and motioned us in. She led the way in silence down a long hallway and into a room which opened off the end of it. When she switched on the light, I saw we had followed her into a small library. She waved us to chairs and went out, slamming the door.

I sat down and lit a cigarette. "A tough hombre. Or should I say hombress? My Spanish isn't so hot."

Katie sat down. I could see she was tense, and I felt the same way. A hundred-grand snatch. A young woman cowering in a gangster hide-out, wondering if she would ever see daylight again. A frantic father fighting to raise the money to buy her back.

Drama? Suspense? Yes, plenty of it, even to Katie and me.

"I guess I was a little rough with Mrs. Barrio," I remarked. "Still, it seemed the only way—"

"She isn't Mrs. Barrio. There isn't any Mrs. Barrio."

"No? Then who's the blonde menace?"

"Housekeeper, most likely."

The door flew open then and Dr. Barrio popped into the room. His hair was wild and so were his black eyes. His face was mottled with red and little beads of sweat stood out on his unusually high forehead. His words were like firecrackers.

"You must go. You must go immediately. You lied to Miss Gregg to get in here. You are not from the police. I know. You are newspaper people. Please get out at once. My daughter—"

ALL AT ONCE he flung into a chair, wringing his hands, gazing at us mutely, his eyes wide and fear-stricken. For thirty seconds he had burned like a piece of celluloid, and then all the fire had gone out of him. He looked, now, like a fragile pile of ash that would collapse if you touched it.

Katie said gently: "You're right, Dr. Barrio. We're newspaper people. But we're not quite as heartless as you seem to think. We haven't published anything about the kidnaping of your daughter and perhaps we never shall. That all depends. We want to talk to you first. We want to help you if we can."

"Help me!" the little Guatemalan groaned. "Can you give me a hundred thousand dollars in cash? Help me, indeed!"

"Now take it easy. Doctor," I urged calmly. "We know how you feel and we know why you're so afraid of publicity. We understand the position this mob has placed you in. But hasn't it occurred to you that you're taking the wrong stand? Hasn't it occurred to you that a lot more is involved in this kidnaping than the safety of your daughter?"

"Have you a daughter?" the little man flashed.

"No, I haven't. And perhaps that's why I get a wider slant on the matter than you do. The way I see it, if you meet the demands of these kidnapers, by refusing to allow publicity and police cooperation, you are encouraging every other mob in the country to make some easy money by pulling a snatch. This is not your problem, Dr. Barrio. This issue in the last few years has became national. Every father and mother in the country who has a few dollars lives today in fear that—"

Well, I went on from there. I gave him half an hour of it, with Katie getting in a few licks when I ran out of breath and arguments. Truthfully, I can't tell you, even now, whether we believed all we said, or whether we were just a pair of selfish, hard-hearted reporters fighting for the right to break a whale of a story. For that matter, our motives aren't important. In the end, certainly they justified the means.

Anyway, after half an hour of verbal fireworks we talked him down. We talked him into thinking it was his duty to the other fathers and mothers of America to give the newspapers a free hand as the only way in which the snatch menace would be successfully fought.

When we had finally convinced him, and calmed him, he told us the story:

Carlotta, who was twenty, had recently come home from finishing school in the East, where she had spent most of the last ten years since the death of her mother. She had very few friends here in the city, and spent much of the time exercising her voice. For diversion, she took long walks into the surrounding hills.

At eight o'clock that morning she had started for a walk. She wore a knitted dress of an unusual shade of pale lavender. She wore low-heeled sandals and a tan beret. When she had not returned by noon the Doctor had become worried. He suggested to his housekeeper, Miss Gregg, that the police be notified. But Miss Gregg, the blonde with the hard eyes, told him not to worry.

AT ONE O'CLOCK a special delivery messenger arrived with a letter.

Dr. Barrio, with trembling hands, took it out of his pocket and showed it to me. It was neatly typewritten and read:

Dr. Barrio:

We have your daughter. She is in a safe place where you cannot find her. You must obey the following instructions implicitly or you will never see Carlota again.

1. Get $100,000 in Federal Reserve Bank Notes, $50,000 in tens and $50,000 in twenties.

2. When you have the money run an ad in the personal column of the *Sentinel* saying you are ready to follow instructions. Address it to Louie and sign it Doc.

3. The bills must not be consecutive. They must be old used bills. They must not be marked. You must not keep a record of the serial numbers of the bills.

4. Have your car ready with plenty of gas. We will tell you what to do.

5. If you notify the police, or if you let this get into the newspapers, or if you try to pull any smart stuff with the bills, everything will be off and Carlota will be killed and that will be that.

Think hard and consider these facts. We have planned this job for years. We are old hands at this racket and know what we are doing. Every move has been figured out and we can't go wrong, if you do as we tell you. If you don't Carlota will suffer.

Louie

Well, we read that over and felt a little sick. Suppose we broke the story and Carlotta turned up floating in the bay? Or dumped out of a car after a "ride?" I tell you, it was something to think about.

I handed the letter back to Dr. Barrio. "Will you be able to raise the ransom?"

He shrugged. "I have virtually nothing. The depression wiped me clean. But I think—I *think*—I have some very good friends. Some of them are in the drawing room now. Others are coming. By tomorrow night—perhaps—"

He was a voluble little man, grief-stricken and excited. Once he got started talking, it was hard for him to stop. He told us of the fortune he had made and lost. He told us how he had hoped, before the crash, to go back to Guatemala and continue his study of the Mayan ruins.

He told us how he had hoped to send his daughter to Vienna to study voice culture. In the last six months things had been picking up a little, perhaps.

"But now," he groaned, "it will take the rest of my life to pay back this money I must borrow. The rest of my life. And maybe that even will not be enough."

The door opened and the blonde stepped in. Her lips twisted and there was a peculiar contempt in her ice-blue eyes as she surveyed Katie and me.

"Don't you think, Doctor, you have talked long enough? Your friends are growing impatient."

He rose quickly, bowed and said: "My housekeeper, Miss Gregg. The gentleman and the lady are from the press."

I stood up and bowed too. Neither Katie nor I nor Miss Gregg said a word. I didn't like the blonde, and I knew damned well she didn't like us. Which made it mutual, and you can't kick at that.

Katie and I got out. We got away from the two of them with a fistful of pictures of Carlotta and without, by some miracle, committing ourselves. We didn't speak until we got back into my car. Then, before starting the motor, I turned to Katie and asked: "Well, how's about it, kid?"

"What do *you* say?"

"Well, suppose we crack the story and the mob lives up to its threat. Would you like to have the murder of that girl on your conscience?"

"You're all wet, Pinky. Every snatch mob makes that threat. Keep mum, or else. But do they carry out their threats? Not ever. At least, hardly ever."

"Hauptmann did."

"HAUPTMANN WASN'T A mob. He was an egomaniac. This is different. Whoever wrote that letter—call him the directing genius of this snatch—is an intelligent man. He realizes there's no point in killing the girl. After he examines the money and finds out it isn't marked and the serial numbers aren't consecutive, he'll turn her loose."

"Perhaps you're right. But if they should kill her—"

"Besides," Katie interrupted. "If we crack the story, and get everybody in the state looking for the mob's hide-out, some flatfoot or apartment manager or country yokel may turn them up. Rescue the girl, collar the mob, save Doc Barrio and his friends a hundred grand. Well, do we shoot the works?"

I sighed. "We shoot the works, Duchess. And I only hope and pray we're right."

Well, we cracked the story, and the town went wild!

The police force got into motion like the old Keystone gang. The sheriff's office took a whirl for themselves. And G-men started dropping out of the sky from every direction. The order was: Stay away from the Barrio home. Give Barrio a chance to contact the kidnapers. But in the meantime, leave no stone unturned in your efforts to locate the hide-out and the girl in the lavender dress.

On the following afternoon a small ad appeared in the personal column of the *Sentinel*. It read:

> LOUIE: Publicity due to circumstances beyond my control. Am complying with instructions. May take several days. Will follow orders implicitly. Please have patience. I will play fair.
>
> DOC.

Three days passed, while our temperatures rose at least a degree every twenty-four hours. The press room was a mad house. Everybody and his brother, it seemed to us who were trying to work, made his headquarters there. The suspense, to put it mildly, was terrific.

Then another ad in the personals:

> LOUIE: Am ready and awaiting further instructions.
>
> DOC.

Meanwhile the various papers in the city had got together with the police and established a field bureau in a vacant house across the street from the Barrio home. Late that night field headquarters simultaneously flashed the detective bureau and the press room: "Special delivery messengers just arrived." And five minutes later: "Dr. Barrio, alone in his car, drove off hurriedly, going north on Linden Street."

I hit a telephone to flash my office with the second message, and then Spike Kaylor and Willie Blake and I started up a little whirlwind and cleaned the press room of everything except working reporters.

"You, Duchess!" Spike growled, when only eight of us were left. "You quit work at six tonight. On your way, sister."

"I'm working, Mr. Kaylor, until Carlotta Barrio is returned to her home."

"Oh, yeah?"

Spike caught her arm. She swung at him. She didn't try to slap him, she tried to slug him in the jaw. Her hard little fist glanced off his ear and for a minute I thought he was going to knock her cold.

WELL, OUR NERVES were pretty taut. I don't remember swinging. All I remember is seeing Spike reel across the room and realizing with a sick feeling of regret that I'd hit him, my best friend. Spike got his balance, started for me with blood in his eye. Then lanky Pete Zerker hopped between us and we stopped squaring off.

"That's a pal for you," Spike said bitterly.

"Well, if you've sunk so low you'd strike a woman—"

"Who struck a woman?"

"You were going to."

"How the hell do you know what I was going to do?"

"Skip it!" Pete Zerker snapped.

Well, we skipped it. But the press room wasn't a very pleasant place as the minutes ticked off into hours and the eight of us settled down for the long wait until Dr. Barrio came home from making the pay-off.

It was two in the morning and we were a weary crowd when we got the flash: "Barrio turning up driveway. Sending a man over now to find out if he made contact."

We waited, sweating. No word from the field headquarters for five minutes, ten, fifteen. Finally Spike Kaylor hurled a telephone book savagely against the wall.

"Do we wait here the rest of the night?" he bellowed.

He grabbed up the telephone and whipped off the receiver. "Spike Kaylor. Who's this?... Pete Moran? Listen, Pete! Whatinell happened to the guy you sent across the street?—Huh? Five minutes ago?—Aw, nuts!"

Spike viciously snapped the receiver on the hook. "Moran says Slim Jenkins came out of Barrio's house five minutes ago, hopped in his car and went off hell bent for election. Now what in the Sam Hill does that mean?"

We didn't know what it meant. Not, at least, for another half hour. Then Captain Wallis, grave and haggard and white, came into the room. We almost mobbed him.

"Spill it, Skipper! Any news?"

The Captain nodded. "Yes, boys. Plenty of news. And all of it bad."

That stopped us in our tracks. We gulped, staring at him. *Plenty of news! All of it bad!*

Katie said quietly: "Go ahead, Captain Wallis."

"Dr. Barrio got his instructions at eleven tonight, as of course you know. He was to drive to the intersection of Highway 99 and Hogan Road, where under a white rock on the right hand side of the road he'd find further directions. He did as he was told. He found the instructions."

Do I have to tell you we were hanging on every word? **"THIS NOTE TOLD** him to drive along Hogan Road for exactly seven and a half miles and then pull off to the side and turn out his lights. This he did. He waited for perhaps fifteen minutes. Then a flashlight shone in his face and a voice said: 'Okay, Doc. Let's have the money.'

"As nearly as Barrio could see, there were three men beside the car. He handed them the package of currency. Two of the men went off into the bushes to count the money, while the third stayed there and kept Barrio covered with the flashlight and a gun. After a few minutes, the other two came back. One of them said, 'Okay, Give it to him.'"

"Give it to him!" Willie Blake gasped.

"Yes. A letter. They passed him a sealed envelope and told him not to open it till he got home, said he'd be watched every foot of the way. So he drove straight home before he looked at the letter."

The Captain took a folded sheet of paper out of his pocket. His voice was low, strained.

"Slim Jenkins just brought it to me. I'll read it to you. It says, 'Doc, we told you you would never see Carlotta alive again if you tried to double-cross us. At six o'clock on the evening we snatched the girl you were in the office of Captain Wallis. The first double-cross. The next morning the papers had complete accounts of what happened. The second double-cross. The serial numbers on the bills you brought us were noted down by eight bank tellers who worked all night in the Anglo Trust Company. The third double-cross. Three times, in our league, is out. The body of your daughter will be found in fifteen feet of water at the southwest corner of Pier 19. Louie.'"

"The dirty, lousy rats!" Pete Zerker snarled.

I leaped for the *Telegram* phone. Five minutes later, when I came out of the booth, Captain Wallis had gone. The others were sitting around staring dumbly at the scarred walls of the press room. No one was saying anything.

I remarked tentatively: "Maybe they were just throwing a scare into Barrio."

"Maybe," Willie Blake said listlessly.

"Perhaps the girl'll turn up in the morning."

"Yeah," Spike Kaylor muttered. "Did you ever see one turn up? You know how they kind of roll over slow-like in the water as the grappling hook brings 'em to the surface?"

"Spike!" Katie screamed.

"You can't take it—can you, Duchess?" Spike jeered.

"But what-the-hell good did it do to kill her?" I persisted. "If we were dealing with a maniac or an eccentric, I'd say maybe they did kill her out of spite. But this snatch showed careful planning. The notes showed intelligence. And intelligent people don't kill young women just out of spite."

Willie Blake stood up, shrugging. "Well, we'll know in the morning."

"Are they going to drag for the body?"

"At daylight. You better be there, Pinky."

"Yeah, Pinky," Spike Kaylor said nastily. "You better be there and see the end of the story. You saw the beginning of it—you and the Duchess."

It was a pretty mean crack. I didn't dare look at Katie or Spike.

"Yes, Pinky," Pete Zerker said resignedly, "if you and the Duchess hadn't cracked the story, the poor girl might be alive today."

I TOOK KATIE'S arm, hauled her out of her chair and made for the door. Another minute with that gang of second-guessers and somebody would get hurt. We got outside without any more cracks and I helped Katie into my car. We were both dead on our feet and plenty sunk.

"I'll take you home, Kid."

I started the car and after a few blocks I said, "Now don't take it to heart, Katie. If the mob actually killed her, they did it because Barrio let the police take the numbers of those bills. They would burn them, because in nine cases out of ten it's the thing that puts the G-men on the trail of snatch mobs."

Katie slumped in the seat; she didn't say anything.

"The publicity didn't do any harm," I said after another block. "Everything went through like clock-work, despite the hue and cry. Everything would have been all right and they'd have got their money and turned Carlotta loose—if the cops hadn't taken those damned serial numbers."

Still she wouldn't say anything.

"Look, kid! I'll offer you ten to three they don't find Carlotta's body when they drag around Pier 19 tomorrow morning."

She came to life then. She gripped my hand hard. She said crisply:

"I'm almost certain you're right, Pinky."

"Atta-girl!" I reached over and patted her hand.

"I'm so certain, Pinky, I'd offer not ten to three but a hundred to one. Carlotta's body won't be found."

Well, that was fine. She sounded plenty confident, a lot more confident than I could feel myself, but that was the way I wanted her to be.

"Look, Pinky! Did you see that note Captain Wallis brought in tonight?"

"Not closely, no. I was phoning my office."

"I saw it closely."

We'd reached her home. I drew up at the curb and glanced around at her. She was looking straight ahead. Her eyes, in the light from the dash lamp, were gleaming. Her lips were thin and set. Something hit me; something hit me hard.

"You saw it closely," I said.

"Yes."

"All right. So what?"

She looked at me and smiled. Then she unlatched the door and stepped onto the curb.

"You were sweet to bring me home, Pinky. Thanks a lot. Will I see you in the morning?"

"Huh? In the morning! Where?"

"At Pier 19. Good night, Pinky."

AT DAYLIGHT THE next morning, in a gray cold drizzle that penetrated clear to the bone, the police started dragging for the body of Carlotta Barrio. We were all there, even Dr. Barrio and Miss Gregg—along with half the population of the city. I found Katie in the mob, pushed through the line the police had drawn and walked with her to the end of the pier.

"How do you feel this morning, kid?" I tried to sound cheerful, just a little ray of sunshine; but with only two hours' sleep and too much coffee the night before. I know my voice was flat and hopeless.

"Fine, Pinky. How are you?" She wasn't chipper, but neither was she sunk.

"I'm great," I said heartily.

"You don't look it. You look like something you find when you turn over a rotten board."

"Well," I sighed, "I wish I could say the same for you. If you had a hard night, no one would know it."

"I haven't slept since the night before last."

"Youth. That's what it is. Youth. What did you do after I brought you home last night."

"I thought."

"All the rest of the night?"

"All the rest of the night."

"What'd you think about?"

"A lot of things."

"Me, perhaps?" The light touch—with two rowboats filled with coppers rowing back and forth at the end of the pier.

"I'm sorry. I didn't give you a thought."

"Do you still think they won't find Carlotta's body?"

"I'm certain they won't."

I turned up the collar of my coat and shivered a little. "Well, I wish I was as sure."

And then a cop in the stern of one of the rowboats raised a shout and started hauling on the line he'd been trailing. The oarsman stopped rowing. The copper with the line heaved it in, slowly and carefully. I don't think anybody on the dock drew a breath for a full minute.

A lavender bundle, like a long narrow sack, rolled up

on the gray oily water. The copper reached down, caught hold of it, jerked his head toward the ladder at the end of the pier. The man at the oars began to row, slowly. The cop in the stern looked up at Captain Wallis, on the dock, and nodded briefly.

I took Katie's arm and said heavily:

"We can skip the rest, kid."

She didn't move.

"You know, Katie, the crabs in this bay can make an unholy mess of a body. You're not morbid. You don't want to look at a thing like that. You'll dream about it for weeks."

They were lifting the body onto the pier. I saw Dr. Barrio drop to his knees beside it. Then I saw him get up, wringing his hands. He was hardly erect before he collapsed in a dead faint.

I jerked Katie's arm. "Are you coming, Duchess?"

She looked up at me. Her eyes were clear and cool. There was no horror in them, no disappointment, no shock. I shivered again; maybe it was the cold wind—and maybe it was the unexpected callousness that shone in Katie Blayne's blue eyes.

"I'm not coming. Pinky. I'll see you in the press room—if you're too squeamish to stay."

Squeamish! Me? As though I'd be bothered by looking at a body on which the crabs had been at work.

I LET GO of her arm, shrugging. "Go ahead, Duchess. Have a good time. I'm glad to find out what kind of a show you enjoy. Next time we want to spend a pleasant afternoon together, suppose we meet at the morgue."

I turned and walked away from her. When I saw her again she was kneeling on the pier beside the body of that poor girl! I almost lost my breakfast. I got out of there and went back to the press room and tried to settle into the routine of stick-ups, burglaries, police courts and auto accidents.

An hour later the dock party was back on the job, all but Katie. No one mentioned Katie and I didn't ask about her. We were a gloomy crowd.

At nine o'clock Captain Wallis came in. We looked up at him but no one asked any questions. We were sick of the whole affair. The G-men were on the job. The serial numbers of the bills had been sent to every bank in the country. Sooner or later, maybe years later, the mob would be smoked out. And that was that, so far as we were concerned.

"Shoot, Skipper!" Spike Kaylor ordered gloomily.

"The medical examiner tells me the girl was killed by a blow at the base of the skull. She's been dead and in the water for about three days."

"Three days!" Willie Blake gasped. "Then—"

Captain Wallis nodded. "The mob never had any intention of returning her alive. They evidently killed her and dumped her the same day they snatched her."

"And that was all—for a while."

Then Katie poked her head in the door and called to me. Although I was thoroughly disgusted with her, I went out into the corridor.

"Well, did you have a nice time picking at the bones?" I asked.

She smiled in a hard, unhumorous way. "I saw," she said, "some fingernails."

"Oh, yes? Well, even a crab will stop at fingernails."

Her lips tightened and her eyes were abruptly cold. "You know, Pinky, you've been pretty nasty to me today. If we hadn't agreed to play fair with each other, I'd tell you to go to hell. It would give me a great deal of pleasure. Did you think I enjoyed looking at that girl's body?"

"You didn't seem to mind it. Tell me more about finger-nails."

"They were short and broken and there wasn't any lacquer on them. Carlotta Barrio kept hers a brilliant vermilion."

WELL, IT SEEMED pretty fantastic. And yet Katie, I knew, isn't one to go off half-cocked. Katie has a mind, she knows how to use it, and she's learned from sad and bitter experience that a young woman reporter should know whereof she speaks before she opens her mouth.

"Are you suggesting they didn't drag Carlotta Barrio out of the bay this morning?"

"Pinky, you're getting positively brilliant."

"Skip the sarcasm and get on with your rat-killing."

"I shall. You saw at least one or those ransom letters, didn't you?"

"Yes. The first one."

"How was the name Carlotta spelled in that letter?"

"Huh?" I scratched my head, feeling sheepish. "I don't know. How was it spelled?"

"Pinky Kane, the observing reporter!" Katie said cuttingly. "Well, I'll tell you, since you've never learned to use your eyes. It was spelled C-a-r-l-o-t-a. With one '*t*.'"

"Well, what of it?" I asked.

"How would you spell it? How would anybody with the intelligence of the person who wrote that note spell it?"

"I'd spell it with two '*t's.*' The same way the papers have been spelling it. But still what of it?"

"Your Spanish, you told me the other night, isn't so hot. Mine, fortunately, is fairly good. In Spanish, Carlota is spelled with one '*t.*'"

"Uh-huh. So what?"

"A Spanish speaking person, or a person who knew the girl was christened Carlota—with one '*t*'—wrote those notes."

I digested that for quite a while—and then my heart began to sound like a freight engine climbing a grade. I looked at Katie; her face was flushed and she was breathing fast.

"Look, kid! Do you want to see this through? With me?"

"With you!" she retorted. "Tell me, Pinky. Who was bright enough to note the spelling of *Carlota* on the note last night and to remember it was spelled the same way in the first note? Who was bright enough to look at that girl's fingernails and see if they were long and narrow and lacquered?"

"Duchess, take a bow. Take two bows. Back in a minute."

I dashed into the press room, pulled a .38 Colt out of my desk and jammed it in my hip pocket. Spike Kaylor jeered:

"And where, Mr. J. Edgar Hoover, are you going with the rod?"

"I'm going out to get the mob that snatched that girl."

And did the gang laugh!

Miss Gregg answered our ring when we reached the Barrio home. I didn't mince matters this time. I shoved her out of the way and walked in, with Katie right at my heels.

"Where's Barrio?" I asked.

"Dr. Barrio," she said stiffly, "is in bed under the care of his physician, who left orders that he was not to be disturbed."

"Well, Gregg, he's going to be disturbed and like it. Where is he?"

"He's upstairs in the room at the head of the hall. And the telephone on which I'll call the police is in the library."

"Call the police and be damned! Come on, Duchess!"

WE RAN UPSTAIRS and left the blonde staring after us with murder in her eyes. We went into the front bedroom and found Dr. Barrio in bed. His face was a greenish-white and he looked pretty sick.

For an instant I was stopped. If Katie and I should be wrong!... But we *couldn't* be wrong!

I closed the door, drew up two chairs beside the bed and sat down.

"Katie, have I heard somewhere that you can take short-hand?"

"Yes."

"Good. Speak slowly, Doc. It'll be easier—for Katie."

He hadn't moved since we burst into the room. He just lay there, looking weak and helpless, his black eyes roving back and forth from Katie to me.

"All right, Doc. Commence."

"What is it," he asked in a feeble voice, "you want me to commence?"

"Listen, Doc. Listen and get this!" I talked pretty rough, I guess, but I kept my voice down so that the blonde, if she was at the keyhole, wouldn't hear what I said. "You're a pretty smart mugg, I guess. You know a lot about Mayas and all that rot. But hasn't anybody ever told you that type-writing is easier to identify than handwriting?"

"Meaning, sir?"

"Doc, you shouldn't have used that typewriter down in the library to write those ransom notes from Louie."

It was a shot in the dark, and plenty long, but I hit the mark. I could tell by the look in his eye, by the way his breathing quickened, by the way his jowls got greener.

"Better get it off your chest, Doc. Where's Carlotta?"

"In Europe."

"How long since."

"She left three weeks ago for Vienna."

"Passport?"

"She took another name, swore falsely to a birth certif-icate. I shall never tell you the name she took."

"But she knew, didn't she, the racket you planned to pull?"

"She knew," Barrio sighed.

"You and the Gregg woman had it all cooked up before she left, didn't you? A hundred thousand dollars! Money donated by your loyal friends. To pay for Carlotta's vocal training and to send you back to Guatemala to learn some more about the Mayas. What was Gregg's cut?"

"She was coming to Guatemala with me."

"Huh! That's what you thought. But we won't go into that. Who's the dame they dragged out of the bay this morning?"

Barrio shuddered. His thin, dark-skinned hands gripped the coverlet, trembling. He moistened his bloodless lips and said, with some spirit: "I swear that was her idea. I didn't want to do it. Cheating my friends, yes. I could do

that—for Carlotta and my studies, for freedom and inde-
pendence in the last years of my life. But murder!" He
groaned. "I tried to talk her out of it. She wouldn't listen
to me. I—I love her—but she's a beast!"

"I said, who was the dame they dragged out of the bay?"
"A GIRL MISS GREGG picked up from the Transient Shelter. A waif who had strayed out here from Nebraska. No
family, no friends. Her first name was Jane. That's all I
know. Gregg brought her here to work as a maid. That
was a week ago." He swallowed hard, fighting for control.
"Oh! What must have gone on that night, down there in
the basement!"

"What night was that?"

"The night before—er—Carlotta disappeared. She
killed her down there, Gregg did. How, I don't know. But
she killed her, after giving her that dress of Carlotta's to
wear. That lavender dress that people had seen Carlotta
walking around the hills in. She made me—help her put
the body in the car and—and drop it off the pier. She made
me, I tell you!"

"Uh-huh. And how much insurance did you have on
your daughter's life?"

"Five thousand dollars."

"Double indemnity for accidental death?"

"I—I think so."

"Uh-huh. Ten thousand dollars. Now why, when you
and Gregg planned to collect a hundred thousand from
your good and loyal friends, did she have to commit this
wanton murder?"

I waited a minute, and when he seemed too distraught
to answer my question, I said: "Never mind. I can dope that

angle myself. It wasn't the ten thousand dollars—though ten G's are ten G's to a dame like Gregg. You needed some clean money to carry you along for a year or two until the ransom bills cooled off.

"You knew the police would insist on taking the serial numbers of those notes. You wouldn't dare cash any of them for a long time. But you needed getaway money. So Gregg cooked up the idea of getting this transient waif and passing off her body as Carlotta's.

"The crabs would take care of identification, all but the teeth. And the only dentist who's worked on Carlotta's teeth was in the East where she went to school.

"Under the circumstances, your identification would be accepted. In fact, it was accepted by everybody but our girl friend here.... Well, have I missed any of the angles?"

"You seem, young man, to have covered everything." Barrio's voice was stronger. "But one thing I must make clear. Carlotta—though she will never be found, had no idea Gregg planned to murder anybody. In fact, I didn't know it myself until after Carlotta had left for Europe."

"That's all right with me. Carlotta is undoubtedly a lousy little tart. But who cares?" I stood up. "Did you get all that, Katie?"

"I got everything, Pinky."

SHE FOLDED HER notes and put them away in her purse. I looked at her for a long minute, trying to make up my mind. Oh, hell, I thought. It costs money to hang people. I took the .38 out of my pocket. I wiped it carefully to get rid of my fingerprints and laid it on the table beside the bed.

"There's a passport, Doc. A passport to hell, or wherever

guys like you end up. There's a bullet in the chamber with your name on it. Come on, Katie. Let's scram."

I walked out of the room without another look at Barrio. Katie came into the hall behind me, and closed the door. She closed the door gently, as though she were leaving a room of the dead. Her face was chalk-white, her teeth were tight on her lower lip and her eyes were shining.

Turning, she ran down the hall to the stairway. I knew she wanted to get away from there as fast as she could; it wouldn't be nice to hear the muffled shot that presently would come from the bedroom.

I caught up with her and we hurried down the stairs together. The blonde was waiting for us at the foot of the steps. I don't think she knew what was up. I'm sure she didn't.

"The police are coming," she said crisply. "You dirty sneaking reporters ought to have more consideration for a sick, heart-broken old man. Can't you give him a break?"

Even then, right up to the last minute, she didn't know what was coming. The .38 barked upstairs. I heard Katie catch her breath in a sob. I saw Gregg's eyes widen and her jaw drop.

I thought of this blonde monster picking out a girl at the Transient Shelter, picking her with an eye to height and build and complexion—and bringing her home to slaughter. Suddenly Katie was so full of pent-up emotion, I knew she'd have to let go. She said, slowly and carefully:

"You said something about giving the old man a break. Well, he's gotten his break. But it's more than I'll give you."

Katie let her have it on the point of the jaw. The blonde

dropped like a log and never moved. Well, it wasn't very nice, but I know I felt a lot better.

"She's on ice till the cops get here," I said. "Come on, Duchess. We'll wait for 'em outside. I think we need some air."